SILENT NIGHT

AN AMBER MCNEIL MYSTERY

SANDRA NIKOLAI

"Hope is the thing with feathers that perches in the soul and sings the tune without the words and never stops at all."
Emily Dickinson, poet (1830–1886)

1

My responsibility this gray Monday morning in November was to choose the next cold case that investigators at Montreal Police Service headquarters would reopen. Selecting one case from more than eight hundred cold cases, contained in dusty bankers boxes in the storage room, was a challenge.

Yet, I was undaunted. As a consultant to investigators in the cold case unit, I was an empath and attuned to capturing eerie sounds and unnerving images emanating from the evidence in these boxes. Not that it got any easier with time. An icy sweat swept over me whenever I visited here, but determination forced me to overcome my fears.

At twenty-five years old, I'd struggled to hide my psychic gift from skeptics for what seemed like forever. But there was a positive side to owning it now. I put it to serious use every time I examined evidence and interviewed potential suspects.

Although my job might appear exciting to outsiders, it had its drawbacks. Unexpected and horrifying impressions surfaced without warning from the evidence, and I had to fight to control my emotional reactions. I often sought refuge in the conference room behind closed doors and away from the rest of the staff so as not to frighten them. In rare instances, what I perceived from the evidence wasn't clear. Experience proved that the passage of time clarified my perceptions. My gift remained a work in progress.

The employees in the cold case unit had eventually come around to accepting the validity of my insights and my spontaneous reactions. They'd promised Lieutenant Albert Payton, our boss, to keep my secret within the boundaries of our team. The lieutenant had cited safety concerns—mine and those regarding the unit—should word get out that the police had hired a psychic consultant. Not to mention the public response it would arouse.

I continued my search down the next aisle. I slid my fingers along rows of boxes stacked on shelves, waiting for a sign that would help me make a choice. It could be an image, a perception, or anything else that a deceased victim might use to get my attention.

An icy blast of wind hit me with a wallop. I stopped, shivering as my fingers rested on a box marked "Susan Kendall, 1983." It was the one! I lifted the box and carried it out of the storage room and down the hallway toward the office.

I passed the conference room and turned the corner into the open office area. Corey Reed and Nadia Paquin, information officers and the youngest members of our team, were busy at their desks.

Tall and slim, Corey greeted me with a hasty "Hey, Amber" before looking back at his computer screen. Nadia gave me her usual deadpan acknowledgment, then glanced away as she continued a phone conversation.

Next up was the lieutenant's glass-walled office. It was empty. He was attending a weekly meeting with city representatives to discuss the recent increase in homicides. On his return, he'd no doubt put pressure on our recently formed unit to solve more cold cases. He often reminded us that the funds to maintain operations—and our jobs—might be cut short if we didn't reach our quota.

Above all, I'd hate to disappoint my uncle, Ted Tremblay, who happened to be chief inspector of the Montreal Police Service. Privy to my secret gift, he'd recommended me for the consultant job to the lieutenant.

I set the box on my desk. The empty chair and tidy desktop to my left indicated that Detective Sergeant Matt Gallo hadn't arrived yet. No surprise. He'd mentioned he had the kids on the weekend and had to drop them off at his ex's this morning.

Detective Sergeant Ryan Baxter, my partner and criminal profiler at the unit, sat at the desk across from mine. He craned his neck around his computer and gave me a quizzical look. "You chose one already?"

"Yes." I smiled. "There's always one that stands out in a special way."

"You're right about that." He smiled back, then puckered his lips and blew me a kiss.

Whenever Ryan flirted with me at work and risked revealing our secret relationship, my pulse quickened. I threw a hurried glace around.

Safe. No one had noticed his behavior. Our jobs were secure.

"I wish you wouldn't do that," I whispered to him, aware that he wouldn't have been so daring if someone had been observing us.

"Do what, Amber?"

His mischievous grin, warm brown eyes, and thick hair made my heart flutter. Our relationship had swiftly progressed from dating to staying the night at my place or his once in a while. Aware that he could get transferred or fired if word got out about our forbidden connection, I was comforted that we trusted each other to keep it under wraps.

I changed the subject. "Ryan, I'd like to go through the evidence in this new case before we discuss it. Okay?"

He gave me an affirmative nod. "Take all the time you need. You'll be in the conference room?" He was well aware that my review of the evidence often resulted in unpredictable reactions.

"Yes." I tucked my phone in my jacket and headed for the secluded room.

Alone behind closed doors, I opened the evidence box. A musty smell sprang from long-abandoned paperwork, filling my nose with a familiar old-book scent. I dug out the folder containing reports filed by police investigators in 1983 and scanned them. Whether it was due to a lack of officers or shrinking department funds at the time, statements covering interviews with witnesses and possible suspects were incomplete or missing. It meant Ryan and I would have to start the investigation into Susan Kendall's murder from scratch.

I removed a newspaper clipping, yellowed with age. The article was published on the first page of the *Willowburg Press* the day after Susan's death and included a photo of the smiling young woman with blonde hair. After the opening paragraph introduced the eighteen-year-old female victim as a former resident, the next section offered more details:

"Police investigators confirm that Susan Kendall's body was discovered frozen the next day after a severe snowstorm. A vagrant had wandered into the alley next to a flower shop and made the grisly discovery. According to an unnamed source, the victim was friendly and bursting with ambition. She quit her job as a waitress at The Easy Diner the day before and was about to start a new life. She never made it.

Willowburg residents were aghast. 'Nothing ever happened like this before,' an elderly woman stammered. 'Who would have done such a thing to this poor young woman, let alone on Christmas Eve?'

The loss of blood from stab wounds allegedly led to the victim's demise, though medical authorities have not yet confirmed the official cause of death. Police have not ruled out foul play and are asking anyone in the area to contact them if they've seen any suspicious activity."

I reached for the autopsy report. It indicated that Susan's body had multiple cuts allegedly made with an eight-inch-blade knife commonly available. Medical authorities couldn't confirm the exact time of death because the cold weather and heavy snowfall had hindered their efforts to do so. They estimated that Susan had died between five in the afternoon and midnight. There were no signs of a struggle, and no evidence was found under her fingernails because she wore woolen mitts. No weapon was found either.

A police investigator's report stated that the perpetrator might have forced the victim into the alley where they would have been hidden from public view. The heavy snowstorm and nightfall would have helped to hide the attack.

I scanned another report detailing Susan Kendall's family history. Her mother had died from a fall down the stairs when Susan was a young teen. Her father was an alcoholic and rumored to have beaten his wife and child, though records show that no charges had been laid against him.

Susan had left home months before she died. Her younger sister, fifteen-year-old Lisa Kendall, had remained with their father. She was Susan's only sibling. When their father could no longer pay for food and other expenses, he handed Lisa over to foster care.

I shuddered. Growing up without parents? I could easily relate to that.

I was five years old when my parents were murdered, and I was adopted by my Uncle Ted and Aunt Elaine. They provided me with a comfortable home, an education, and fun outings. Because of my sensitivity to loud noises and busy environments, they understood my need for alone time. As a result, books often topped my gift requests on special occasions and were delivered in abundance.

I felt a twinge of guilt. Loving family members had taken care of me when other children hadn't been as lucky. The painful reality? Life wasn't necessarily fair.

I retrieved three transparent evidence bags from deep inside the bankers box and sat down. One contained an empty matchbook, another a cigarette stub, and the last one, three burnt matches. DNA testing hadn't existed back then, so no reports from forensics were available.

I pulled on a pair of vinyl gloves and removed the matchbook. The Easy Diner was the name on the cover. Scribbled in ink on the inside were names and phone numbers. One of the names was Lisa. Probably Susan's sister. The other names listed were Debra, Kenneth, diner, and home. As I held the matchbook, I perceived a cacophony of voices too numerous to distinguish, like a group of people talking loudly at a party. I returned the matchbook to the evidence bag.

Next up was the cigarette stub. I'd barely held it when I captured an image of a man rushing toward me with a knife. His features weren't clear because his face was contorted in anger. My pulse accelerated. Was he Susan's murderer?

I hastily dropped the cigarette stub into the bag. After taking a deep breath to calm down, I reached for the burnt matches in the third bag. I perceived the same image of an extremely angry man with a knife. He was charging right at me!

"No!" I jerked backwards and fell out of my chair. I regained my balance and clasped the amethyst crystal in my pocket to lessen my angst. It was a gift from my Aunt Elaine who shared the same psychic lineage as me.

There was a hard knock at the door.

I righted the chair and composed myself. "Yes?"

Ryan peeked inside, his forehead lined with worry. "Are you okay, Amber? Your scream scared the heck out of us."

"Yes, I'm okay."

"Are you sure?"

"I already said I was okay." I softened my tone. "I just need to be alone for a little while longer, Ryan."

"You got it." He smiled and shut the door.

I sat down and mentally replayed the elements in Susan's case:

A young woman's death.

A cruel father.

A snowstorm.

Christmas Eve.

Burnt matches.

A frozen body found in an alley the next day.

I'd read enough stories in my youth to recognize that the details in Susan's case reminded me of one of Hans Christian Anderson's fairy tales published centuries ago. In "The Little Match Girl," a poor young girl tries to sell matches in the street on a snowy and freezing New Year's Eve. She's afraid to go home because her father beat her if she failed to sell any. Ignored by pedestrians, she huddles in an alley and lights matches to keep herself warm. In the flame, she sees a vision of her late grandmother, the only person who treated her kindly. When the matches burn out, her grandmother carries her soul to heaven. The girl's frozen body is discovered the next morning.

Ryan and I had investigated cold cases where an abductor used fairy tales as his mantra to "save" the children and later killed them. I questioned whether Susan's murderer fell into a similar category. Then again, maybe my imagination was working overtime.

I was putting the items back in the evidence box when I detected another transparent bag at the bottom. I'd almost missed it. It contained a blurred black-and-white Polaroid photo. No date or other reference was inscribed on the front or back of it. A sudden feeling of dread engulfed me. The image of a young woman screaming in horror flashed before me, then vanished in the next moment.

I peered closer at the photo and trembled. It was an ultrasound image of a baby!

Was Susan pregnant when she died? If so, this revelation would put a whole new slant on our investigation.

2

I strolled past Corey and Nadia who gave me wide-eyed stares from behind their computer screens. I smiled apologetically. It was clear they'd need more time to get fully accustomed to my sudden outbursts.

Sitting at the desk across from mine, Ryan stood as I approached. "What did you get from the evidence, Amber?"

I set the bankers box on my desk. "I got an insight that was so true to life that it terrified me." I described what I'd seen.

"He could be the perp who murdered Susan Kendall," he said.

"I had the same insight twice. What's worse, he's alive!"

He gaped at me. "You're kidding."

"No. I couldn't get a clear image of his face, though. Only that he was so angry. Sorry." I bit my lip to suppress the strong disappointment that surged inside me.

Ryan reacted as I'd expected. "It's early yet. We'll figure things out. We usually do. Stop being so hard on yourself, Amber."

He was hinting at the single event in my life that still affected me, and he was right. Although I was a young child when my parents were murdered in our home, I hadn't been able to shake the guilt of having been spared the same fate. When the intruder had broken in, I'd hidden in a safe spot that my father had built for me. Our upscale neighborhood had been the target of recent home invasions, and my safety was my parents' utmost concern. Since the incident, guilt swept over me more often than I cared to admit. Working on cold cases and helping to nab the bad guys gave me a way to confront my ghosts and offer an atonement of sorts.

I handed Ryan the file containing the witness reports. "There's not much information in here that can help us find Susan Kendall's killer."

He spread the reports out on his desk and gave them a quick perusal. He sighed. "Looks like we have our work cut out for us."

"You have a problem with my choice of a case?" I teased him.

"Not at all. If you picked this case, we'll solve it. Right?" He raised a thumb.

"Right." I was determined, not only to prove that I could continue to contribute to the investigative unit but also to justify my Uncle Ted's endorsement of my capabilities. My hiring through an inside channel was a well-kept secret. Only Ryan and the lieutenant knew about it. My privileged connection reinforced my resolve to succeed even more.

Ryan pulled on a set of vinyl gloves. He walked over to my desk and carefully handled the items in the evidence box. "Okay. Sum it up for me, Amber."

I briefed him on the case and the images I'd perceived from the evidence. Although our approaches differed, we'd grown to respect each other's interpretations. Most of the time, anyway.

"The ultrasound photo was a big surprise," I said. "Unless the father is still alive and comes forward, we might never find out who he was."

"More importantly, was he the killer?" He raised an

eyebrow. "I'll send the photo to forensics ASAP. They should be able to lift DNA and prints off it." He studied the burnt matches. "I'll send these to forensics too. Maybe our perp was a smoker. Why he'd leave burnt matches behind is a curious gesture."

"A symbolism of sorts?" I suggested.

"Could be." Ryan inspected the matchbook cover. "I'll give the names and phone numbers listed here to Corey for follow-up."

"Can we trace the source of the ultrasound photo?"

"It would be useless," he said. "Medical records are kept for ten years, then destroyed."

"I want to find out more about the town where Susan lived." I did a quick Google search on my computer. "Willowburg is located in the west area of Montreal, about twenty miles from here. It has a population of a thousand people. Where everyone knows everyone else, as they say. We don't know who Susan's doctor was, but someone else must have known about her pregnancy."

"Even so, it won't help our investigation unless they're willing to talk." Ryan discarded his gloves in the wastebasket.

"What do you mean?"

"Small-town residents are good at keeping secrets."

I'd only lived in a big city, so I was curious about his claim. "How do you know that?"

He shrugged. "Experience. When I worked in homicide, we frequently tracked suspects to outlying towns. People there were afraid to talk, even if they had information that could help the police arrest the perps."

I had another question. "What about surveillance cameras in the town?"

"They weren't as widespread in small towns as in cities back then. Even today, certain towns in Quebec have limited street patrols from the provincial police who oversee them." He moved to his desk and fingered the reports. "Let's review what we know about our potential witnesses."

"Bill Hardy was the owner of The Easy Diner in Willowburg," I said. "He was about forty years old back then. He was probably the last person to see Susan alive before she quit her job that afternoon and left."

Ryan scanned the report. "Bill Hardy didn't say why she quit her job. Or it's possible the investigator didn't ask. There might be a lead there." He picked up another report. "What about Debra Robinson?"

"She worked as a waitress with Susan at the diner. Susan roomed at her apartment for a short while. Debra was about thirty years old and is one of the names listed on the matchbook cover."

"Uh-huh. A coworker and a close friend. Another possible lead." He picked up the last report. "Kenneth Cameron. Twenty-one years old."

"He was Susan's boyfriend. He was supposed to meet her after work but was delayed. When he got to their meeting place, she wasn't there."

"The prospective father of her child?" Ryan suggested.

"Maybe," I said. "When we interview him, we can ask him if he ever saw the ultrasound photo of the baby before."

"That's not the best idea."

"Why not?"

"I'd like to keep the photo a secret from him for a while longer."

"You mean, in case Kenneth offers us that bit of information first?"

"Correct. If he doesn't, it could mean he has something to hide." Ryan flipped through other sheets in the folder. "There are no other witness reports here. I'd have expected one on Richard Kendall, Susan's father. On her sister, Lisa, too."

"Lisa was in foster care at the time," I said. "Those records are hard to access."

"True." He gathered the papers. "I'll get Corey and Nadia to try to locate these witnesses and set up meetings. Without their statements, I'm afraid we won't get very far."

Considering the scarcity of solid evidence, I was eager to meet with the witnesses in person. It was a chance to gain insights from them that might help to identify the horrific killer. Above all, I was counting on Ryan to continue to trust my perceptions. Without his belief in my abilities, I feared the scant evidence in this case would only lead us to a dead end.

3

———————

The clinking of a hanger on a rack and the thump of winter boots dumped at the entrance of the unit filtered down the hallway, followed by the heavy padding of shoes.

Matt rounded the corner, a large mug of coffee in his hand. As he came up to us, he said, "Sorry I'm late. My ex-wife wanted me to drop the kids off at school, not her place. What's up?"

"Grab a chair," Ryan said. "We're working on a new case."

Matt wheeled his chair closer to us and sat down. "Who's the victim?"

"Susan Kendall." Ryan briefed him on the main details on file. "The evidence surrounding her death isn't much to go on, but one good lead is all we need to crack the case."

Matt grinned. "Unless Amber works her magic, you mean." He winked at me.

I bristled at his comment. "It's not magic."

Matt grimaced. "Whatever." He drank some coffee.

Despite sharing my deepest secret with him and the rest of the staff at the unit, Matt doubted my abilities more than anyone else. At least I could count on Ryan.

"These copies are for your review, Matt." Ryan handed him

photocopies of the police reports. "Nadia and Corey will try to get locations on the witnesses interviewed in the past. In the meantime, we need someone to branch out from here." He kept his eyes on him.

"Okay." Matt did a double take. "Wait a minute. Branch out? Is that what I think it means?"

Ryan nodded. "You're already familiar with the process. Scope out the boundary around the crime scene. Knock on doors and interview the locals. Willowburg is a small town, but a number of residents from the 1980s might still be living there. See what you can find out."

"Why do I have to do the legwork in every case?" Matt grumbled.

Ryan leaned forward. "Amber and I will interview the witnesses. There could be more of them than we think. These cold cases have legs."

"Fair enough. When do I start?"

"Now would be a good time," Ryan said. "They forecast a heavy snowfall this afternoon. It'll get messy driving on the roads later."

Matt stood up. "Say no more. I'm on it." Coffee cup in hand, he headed out.

Corey hurried up to Ryan and me minutes later. "I located Dr. Kenneth Cameron in Montreal. I was able to book your meeting with him for Wednesday afternoon."

"In two days." Ryan took note of it on his phone.

"He was busy and couldn't meet with you before then." Corey adjusted his glasses, a nervous habit whenever he was stressed.

"That's okay."

Corey went on. "As far as doctors go, his patients gave him a very favorable rating online. I thought I'd mention it as a point of interest. I'll continue searching for the other names on your list."

"If your general searches don't pan out, search the criminal database and the obituaries. Hospitals don't maintain records past ten years, so a search there won't lead anywhere."

"Okay. I'm covering incoming calls on the Info-Crime line today, so Nadia is giving me a hand in locating the other names. I'll let her know." He scooted off.

"Thanks, Corey," Ryan said to his back.

Not to be outdone, Nadia arrived on Corey's heels. "I was able to confirm Debra Robinson's location. You have a meeting with her early this afternoon at one. Is that okay?"

"Yes, thanks," Ryan said, adding a note on his phone. He waited until she'd walked away, then turned to me. "We have interviews scheduled with two witnesses so far. It's a good start." Yet a flicker of doubt in his eyes negated his positive comment.

"What's wrong?" I asked.

"We've learned a lot from the cold cases we've solved. We should speed things up and follow the same wide strategy if we want to succeed with this one as well."

"You mean, ask the public for help?"

"Exactly. Corey and Nadia can easily set up the victim's page on our police website. They're busy uploading hundreds of cold case files into the system and handling other things, but we need their help ASAP."

"Let's ask them now," I said.

We met briefly with the duo at their desks to discuss our plans. "I hate to switch gears like this, but putting Susan Kendall's page up for public viewing is a vital step in our investigation," Ryan explained.

"Not a problem," Nadia said in her no-nonsense manner. "We enjoy working on projects that tap into our creativity."

Corey's face lit up. "That's right. We welcome any break

from our routine responsibilities." He adjusted his glasses. "I mean, it's not that we don't like the usual work, it's just that—"

"It's okay, Corey," Ryan said, smiling. "We get it."

Annoyed with her slightly younger colleague, Nadia gave her head a tiny shake. "Is there anything we should focus on, Ryan?"

"You have the basic information we gave you for Susan Kendall, so go ahead and set up her page. Amber and I will provide additional details as we proceed with our investigation. Prepare the usual press release asking for the public's help. Withhold details about the physical evidence from the public, specifically the three matches and the ultrasound photo."

"We'll try to locate friends that Susan attended high school with and get school photos for you," I said.

"That's all for now," Ryan said to them. On the way back to our desks, he said to me, "Next on our agenda is our interview with Debra Robinson. Should be interesting."

"I can't wait to meet with her," I said. "She probably knows more about Susan's last days than anyone else does."

4

The three-story apartment block in Willowburg could have been designated as a heritage building, like most of the structures in this quaint town bordered by thick forests. Built in the sixties, it had a brown brick façade and tall narrow windows overlooking the town square where a towering Christmas tree now stood.

Debra Robinson lived in one of the apartments on the second floor. The seventy-two-year-old woman with curly gray hair invited Ryan and me into her living room. "Please, sit down." She gestured toward a blue velvet sofa that had seen better days.

Ryan began the interview with a general question to put Debra at ease, like he did with all his witnesses. "How long have you lived here in Willowburg?"

"All my life. It's one of the safest towns around. It helps that I know almost everyone who lives here. In fact, this apartment has been my home, like forever." Her smile softened the wrinkles on her face.

"We understand you once worked at The Easy Diner. Tell us about it."

"Oh, it was a hectic place. People loved eating there. They certainly kept the place hopping. And me." She giggled.

"It must have been hard to make enough money as a waitress to support yourself," Ryan said. "How did you manage?"

"I worked long hours and extra shifts. We all did. It was against the law, but who noticed?" When Ryan said nothing to refute her statement, she said, "The owner of the diner was okay with us working extra hours. Besides, it paid my rent and the bills."

I entered the conversation. "As you know, we're investigating the murder of Susan Kendall. Can you tell us about her?"

"Oh my goodness." Debra sighed. "It seems like yesterday, but I can still remember that sweet girl. Suzie—it was my nickname for her—started working in the spring as a waitress at the diner. She was the youngest in the group, but she worked so hard, like all we girls did. She often said she wanted to make a better life for herself. But it didn't happen for her." Her blue eyes watered.

I felt her sadness but pushed forward. "Did she ever confide in you about her personal life?"

"Oh yes. She told me she was going through a rough patch at home. Her father demanded she hand over her pay and tips every week. He'd get angry and beat her if he thought she was holding back on him."

I compared that detail once again to the abusive father in the fairy tale, "The Little Match Girl." It was too similar to ignore.

Debra continued to vent, as if she were relieved that someone had finally given her the opportunity to do so. "Whenever we saw Suzie steal bites from leftovers that clients didn't eat, we girls bought her a sandwich or a coffee. Willowburg had no bus service, so one of the older girls gave her a lift to and from work. It was a short drive. Otherwise, Suzie would have to walk to work along a country road in all kinds of bad weather. She finally got wise and hid her tips from her father.

At least she was able to save some money. When she turned eighteen, she left home."

Ryan resumed his questioning. "Debra, you said Richard Kendall was rumored to be a violent man. Can you tell us more about him?"

She shook her head. "They weren't rumors. Everyone knew he beat his wife. Many times. Bruises don't lie. She was obviously afraid to report him to the police. The last I heard was that she fell down the basement stairs and died. I don't believe it for a minute."

"Why not?"

"Her husband was a selfish brute. Don't get me started." She clenched her jaw.

"Do you know where Richard is now?"

"Someone told me he was in a long-term care home in Verdun, south of Montreal," Debra said. "I forgot the name of the place."

Ryan tapped a note on his phone. "Any next of kin that you know of?"

"No, except for Lisa, his other daughter."

"Do you know how to reach her?"

"No. She moved away long ago. I don't know where she lives." Debra's gaze wandered around the room, as if she were recalling other memories. "Suzie felt awful about leaving her sister behind with that monster of a father. I can't say for sure if he ever laid a hand on Lisa. I hope he didn't." Her forehead furrowed. "At least, not that anyone noticed."

A thought popped into my mind: *Emotional bruises never leave physical scars.*

Even though I knew the answer to my next question, I had to hear it from her. "Debra, did Susan live with you in this apartment?"

"Yes, but not for long," she said. "I let her stay here for a small fee."

"Do you remember the last time you saw her?"

Debra's expression hardened. "It was the day she had an argument with Bill and quit her job."

"It sounds as if they didn't get along."

She stiffened. "You could say that."

Her body language told me we'd hit a nerve.

Ryan took the cue. "How well did you know Bill Hardy?"

Debra joined her hands in a tight grasp. "Very well. I worked at his diner for more than ten years."

"Did his employees get along with him?"

"Well..." She hesitated. "He was pleasant with everyone. He often sang along to some of the songs that played on the vintage jukebox while he worked. The clients enjoyed the friendly atmosphere, but it didn't stop the staff turnover."

"Staff turnover?" Ryan repeated.

"Most of the young girls quit after a few months. Working as a waitress at The Easy Diner was their first job after high school."

"They quit because they got better jobs elsewhere?"

Debra pressed her lips together. "No, they quit because Bill was a persistent flirt. A womanizer. He didn't leave those poor girls alone. Traveling to a job in a big city was expensive. They had no choice but to work in a town that offered jobs to inexperienced young people. They toughed it out as long as possible to show they had work experience."

"Since Bill was a womanizer," Ryan said, "how did that work out for you?"

"I was dating one of his close friends, so he didn't bother me. As for the other girls, I protected them as much as I could. Many of them gave in to his advances. They didn't want to get fired." She huffed. "At one point, I'd seen enough. I stepped in."

"What did you do?"

"I was thirty years old and felt like a mother hen to each new arrival. I told Bill to stop chasing after the young girls."

"Did he listen to you?"

"No." Debra wrung her hands. "Bill had a horrible temper.

He told me to mind my own damn business and that I could quit my job, if I wanted. Of course, I couldn't afford to."

I asked her, "Did Bill flirt with Susan too?"

"My heavens, yes," she said. "I'm sure it's one of the reasons she stopped working there. Another reason was that Suzie had often asked for a raise, but Bill had refused her every time."

I guided the conversation back to an earlier topic. "Did anything out of the ordinary happen on the last day Susan worked at the diner?"

"Yes. Like I told you before, it was the argument she had with Bill."

"What was it about?"

"I don't know," Debra said with a shake of her head. "It was around five that afternoon. We were really busy with customers. Devon, the assistant cook, was hustling orders in the kitchen. Bill wasn't around. When I asked him where Bill was, he said he was arguing with Suzie in the back room. It's right off the kitchen. Anyway, I'm sure they weren't arguing about a raise since Suzie told me she was quitting her job that very day. She'd packed up her things at my place the night before."

"Did she talk to you before she left the diner?"

"No. I was shocked. She ran out crying without saying goodbye to anyone. When the diner closed later that night, my boyfriend picked me up. We went to a party at a friend's house, but I couldn't stop thinking about Suzie. Then the next day..." She choked on her words.

I asked the ultimate question. "Debra, do you have any idea who would have killed Susan?"

"Rumors were that a drifter killed her...that there was no threat to the town."

A wave of fear rolled over me. Debra's fear. She was being evasive and substituting hearsay instead of saying what she truly believed.

Ryan ignored her comment. "Were there any customers that

Susan might have rubbed the wrong way? Someone who had flirted with her?"

"Not really," Debra said. "The customers loved Suzie. Everyone knew everyone in town, so Suzie called each customer by their first name. It made them feel at home." She stared into the distance. "Of course, there were a couple of young men who teased her about how pretty she was, how come she wasn't married, and so on, but Suzie handled herself well."

"What about other male employees at the diner?"

"Oh... I almost forgot about Devon Hill, the assistant cook. He liked Suzie. He was seventeen and shy. Quite harmless. Bill made him work extended hours, often without pay. He accused Devon of sloppiness in the kitchen and yelled at him. He pushed him around a lot."

"How?"

"He poked him in the shoulder and stuff. Devon was as tall as Bill but leaner. I expected the kid to defend himself, but he needed the job, so he didn't fight back or say anything that would get him fired. He worked there for about six months. The day after Suzie was killed, he quit without a word to anyone. I have no idea where he went."

Ryan noted Devon's name on his phone. "You mentioned that you worked at the diner for ten years. Did you leave on good terms with Bill?"

"I had no choice. To leave, I mean. The economy went downhill. Bill had to sell the diner. The buyer was going to tear down the place and build a condo. Of course, we all lost our jobs." She raised her chin. "In the end, though, Bill got his just desserts."

"What do you mean?"

"A couple of years before he sold the diner, Bill had earned an award as the best employer in Willowburg for high school grads. Give me a break." She pushed back a lock of gray hair from her forehead. "Payback time came when he lost his business."

"Is there anything else you'd want to tell us about Bill?" Ryan asked.

"I already told you what I know. You'll have to figure out the rest." She folded her arms and stared at the floor. "I have nothing more to say."

Ryan waited. It was his strategy to get witnesses talking, but Debra remained silent.

As far as body language went, her attitude didn't fool me. She was scared. I couldn't blame her. Retaliation for telling the truth can come at a high price.

5

———

Ryan was patient but persistent in drawing more information from Debra Robinson. He tried a different approach and asked about the other men in Susan Kendall's short life. "We understand that Susan had a boyfriend."

Debra's mood lightened up and she smiled. "Yes. Kenneth Cameron. He was studying to be a doctor. Handsome guy. He came to the diner twice a week and left Suzie generous tips. Of course, he could afford it. He came from a rich family."

"Was it a serious relationship?" I asked her.

"Oh yes. Suzie told me he was her first true love. I was so happy when she said they were going to get married." She paused. "Until I wondered how Kenneth's family would react."

"What do you mean?"

Debra leaned forward a little. "The gossip in town was that his family wasn't keen on him dating Suzie. If Kenneth married her, it would hurt the family reputation. It's the old story: Rich boy marries poor gold digger. Like I said, it was gossip. Rich people know how to cover up their mistakes, with money anyway."

I assumed her last comment about rich people came from

hearsay too. I moved on. "You said Kenneth was studying to be a doctor. Since he and Suzie were unemployed, how were they going to manage financially?"

"I asked Suzie about that," she said. "She told me Kenneth had a trust fund in his name that the family had provided for him when he turned twenty-one. He was already twenty-one."

"So, they were planning to leave town that night," I prompted her.

"Yes. Suzie told me they wanted to get married in a private ceremony out of town. It didn't surprise me. Kenneth's family not being involved with the wedding, I mean."

"Why wouldn't they be involved?"

"I'd heard that Kenneth had a falling out with his parents, that they..." Debra stopped. "Forgive me for saying this, but I believed Suzie was pregnant. They might have been leaving town to save their families the embarrassment."

What a disclosure!

Ryan and I had withheld the physical evidence about Susan's pregnancy from the public. Now Debra had outdone us with her revelation. Yet, I had to be sure. "What made you assume Susan was pregnant?"

"After witnessing her bouts of morning sickness for days on end, I figured she had to be," she said with a shrewd expression.

"Did you tell Susan you thought she was pregnant?"

"Yes, I did. She said no, she had a digestive problem. In other words, it was none of my business. The news about her murder didn't mention she was pregnant, so I guess I was wrong after all."

I held back from telling Debra the truth. If I'd anticipated that she could confirm who the baby's father was, that notion promptly evaporated.

Ryan asked her, "Do you happen to have a picture of Susan? We can post it on the police website and ask the public for information to help us find the killer."

"Yes, in fact, I do." Debra made her way to a desk by the

window and opened a drawer. "This is a photo of Suzie and me taken at my birthday party at the diner after hours. It's the only one I have of her." She held out a creased Kodak photo. "Cell phones didn't exist back then." She shrugged apologetically.

Ryan took hold of the photo. It was a safeguard to prevent me from taking it and reacting to it in front of Debra. "Thank you." He glanced at it, then slipped it in an evidence bag he retrieved from his coat. He routinely carried a supply in case.

"Debra, is there anything else you can tell us about Susan that could help our investigation?" I asked.

"Not really." She heaved a deep sigh. "To this day, I feel guilty for not having protected her. What a terrible ending to that poor girl's life. My heavens!" She blinked, holding back tears. "I'm so glad I helped her when she was going through a rough time."

Her pain and sadness enveloped me. I slipped a hand into my pocket and fingered the amethyst crystal to calm my emotions.

Despite sharing her feelings with us, Debra had remained elusive about naming possible suspects. Maybe she had a good idea who Susan's killer was but was too frightened to tell us. Was it a valid reason to hold back information? If she believed the killer was alive and a threat to her, maybe it was.

6

As soon as we returned to the unit, Ryan asked Corey to track down Richard Kendall's location. Based on the tip from Debra, he lived in a long-term care facility in Verdun, a Montreal borough.

I sat at my desk across from Ryan as he entered a report on our meeting with Debra into a computer file. "She's one secretive lady," I said to him. "I'm sure she's holding back information."

"My gut told me so too," he said. "If her guilt complex kicks up a notch, she might decide to cooperate with us." He stopped tapping on his keyboard and handed me the evidence bag containing the photo Debra had given us. "In the meantime, see if you get anything from this."

I studied the photo. A smiling Debra and Susan stood next to each other. A birthday cake with lots of candles sat on a table before them. Other employees stood behind them, some laughing, others making silly faces. "Debra and Susan look like best friends. Their happy expressions are genuine."

"Anything else?"

"Someone's missing in the picture."

"The photographer?" Ryan joked.

"Very funny." I gave him a wry smile. "Seriously, I get the impression the photographer is quite happy about taking the photo."

"Anything else?"

"No. Sorry."

"Hang onto it. Corey can upload it to Susan's page on the police website later."

As I pondered the items in Susan's evidence box, a memory resurfaced. "Ryan, do you remember how Debra said Susan's father expected her to hand over her pay and tips?"

He tapped on the keyboard without glancing up. "Uh-huh. What about it?"

"It's one more similarity to 'The Little Match Girl.' What if we're searching for another serial killer with a penchant for fairy tales?"

"If you're saying our perp is like the other fairy-tale serial killers we put away, you're wrong. In fact, I doubt we're looking for a serial killer."

"Why not?"

Ryan peeked at me from behind his computer. "Serial killers prefer to stay in their comfort zone. They don't venture far from where they live. They usually stake out a victim within a mile or so from their own home."

"What about the body?" I asked. "Do they usually dump the body close to home too?"

"Statistics show they leave their victim's body not more than twenty miles away. As for the case we're investigating, I checked. No other murders were committed within a twenty-mile range of Willowburg over that same ten-year period."

"In other words, you're concluding that Susan's murder was a one-time incident and that a serial killer wasn't involved."

"Correct. On the other hand, I can't discount the serial killer theory completely. There are exceptions."

"Aren't you contradicting yourself?"

"Not really," Ryan said. "The point is these guys don't always stick to the rules."

I let the argument go. Although my instincts told me we were definitely dealing with a serial killer, we needed to find him before we labeled him.

Another memory gnawed at me. "I wished we could have shown Debra the ultrasound photo of Susan's baby. She seemed to know a lot about her."

"We agreed to keep this detail hidden for now," he said. "It's an ace up our sleeve. We can't trust anyone to find out about her pregnancy. At least, not until we interview all our witnesses."

While he took a phone call, I retrieved the ultrasound photo from the evidence box. I struggled between fighting off the horrid image of Susan being attacked and wanting to see the attacker more clearly. But to no avail.

No sooner had Ryan ended his phone conversation than Lieutenant Payton approached us to get a briefing on Susan Kendall's case. It was standard procedure for our boss to stay informed about ongoing cases. In turn, the lieutenant reported our progress to his superiors and maintained funding for the unit. Of course, additional funding—and our survival—depended on how successful we were in solving more cold cases.

The lieutenant listened attentively as Ryan briefed him, then said, "City councillors are concerned about the recent increase in gun violence. Homicide is having a hard time keeping up with current murder investigations. I'd hate to pull you off this case to meet the shortfall over there."

Ryan hid his astonishment behind a calm exterior. "Sir, we have more witnesses lined up in Susan Kendall's case. We have a lot more ground to cover."

The lieutenant nodded. "Keep following the trail. We need to meet that quota in cold case resolutions." He checked his watch. "I'm off to a meeting with other lieutenants. You know how to reach me."

Ryan gave me a ride home after work. My car was acting up, so I left it in the parking lot behind headquarters.

He steered his car carefully through snow that had already accumulated in the streets. The snow was predicted to intensify to a blustery blizzard overnight. It meant that morning drivers would have to battle high drifts and dangerous driving conditions if snowplows couldn't keep up with cleaning the streets.

The weather reminded me of the snowstorm the night Susan Kendall was killed. I put myself in her shoes and imagined the horror she'd experienced. If she'd expected Kenneth to show up at their meeting place, she must have been shocked at the surprise arrival of her killer instead.

Or maybe she wasn't surprised. Her murderer might have been someone she knew and had no reason to fear, a familiar face who had followed her there, or someone simply asking for directions.

Since Susan Kendall had sent me a plea for help, I vowed to find out the truth. No matter what.

7

Thick snowflakes, scattered by gusty winds, created whiteout conditions and reduced visibility as Ryan and I drove to work the next morning. It was the snowstorm they had forecast. Car accidents punctuated the slushy roads, impatient motorists honked their frustration, and pedestrians huddled at bus stops like white-sheathed mummies.

Ryan charged through a mound of snow left by a snowplow at the entrance to the parking lot at police headquarters. After he parked, we trudged through banks of the white stuff to the door. Luckily, I'd worn knee-high winter boots. Ryan's boots weren't as tall, and he gathered snow on his pant legs that he'd have to shake off indoors.

More heaps of snow would soon pile up around the cars in the parking lot, including mine that I'd abandoned the night before. What if it wouldn't start at the end of the day and I'd need to call a towing company? I dreaded to think that far ahead.

In the hallway, we removed our wet coats and boots and stopped by the kitchen for coffee. Thankfully someone had made a fresh pot.

Ryan poured coffee into two cups, then took a sip of his. "We're lucky we don't have any interviews scheduled today. There's no way we'd be able to drive around the city in this weather."

"I'm hoping my car will start later." I wrapped my fingers around my cup of coffee, feeling the warmth penetrating them.

"Don't worry," he whispered. "I'm here for you." He leaned over and kissed me on the lips.

"Oh! Wait a sec." I grabbed a paper napkin from the counter and wiped a smudge of my lipstick from his lips. "Let's head for our desks before we get into more trouble."

As we turned the corner into the open office area, Corey had news for us. Based on the tip from Debra, he was able to target his search and locate Richard Kendall. "He's living in a facility called Starlight Nursing Home. I scheduled a meeting with him in two days. I'll send you a message with the details."

"Good job," Ryan said.

"There's more," Corey said, confidence in his voice. "I found Bill Hardy in the criminal database. He had a speeding violation months ago. I set up a meeting with him for tomorrow. I hope that's okay, with the weather and all that." He gestured toward the windows and the view of a lashing snowstorm.

"We'll be okay," Ryan said. "The storm should die down, and the city will clean up the streets overnight." He led the way to our desks.

"I'm glad you're so optimistic," I said to him as we took our seats across from each other. "They forecast another foot of snow. How are we supposed to get home later?"

"Maybe we won't." He grinned, a twinkle in his eyes.

Matt arrived at the unit in the early afternoon. His hair was flattened from having worn a knit cap, and his face was red from the whipping winds. "Hope you guys aren't planning to head out again soon. It's wild out there. Me and three other guys helped push a car out of a heap of snow that the driver had skidded into."

"We have no more interviews scheduled for today," Ryan said from behind his desk.

"I'm beat." Matt placed his phone and an oversized cup of coffee on his desk and slumped into a chair. "I spent hours visiting the Willowburg neighborhood around Susan Kendall's old home."

Ryan rose from his chair and rounded our desks. "Did you find out anything worthwhile?"

Matt took a sip of coffee. "Yep. Two residents claim the Kendall family was religious and attended Mass every Sunday. Richard was a hard worker until his wife died, then he hit the bottle more than before. Rumors were that he had become violent over the years. Your witness mentioned that, right?"

"Right," Ryan said. "Debra Robinson told us Richard was a violent father and husband."

Matt continued. "He had debts piling up and sold the house the kids had grown up in. Authorities placed Lisa, the youngest daughter, in foster care at that point. Susan had already moved out. She was eighteen."

"Any known address for Lisa?" Ryan asked him.

"Not yet. Corey is doing a search." Matt picked up his phone and scrolled through his notes. "Several of the neighbors barely knew Susan's mother. One woman who attended the same church noticed bruises on her arms. She told me Mrs. Kendall cleaned people's homes for a living and thought she was acci-dent prone." He looked up at us. "The story goes that she fell down the stairs in their home and broke her neck. Makes you wonder if it was an accident, huh?"

"I don't want to jump to conclusions," I said, "but it sure doesn't help to paint a positive picture of Richard Kendall."

"Let's keep him in mind." Ryan guided things along. "Any-thing else?" he asked Matt.

"Yep. I visited the site where the old diner used to be. An older resident told me the building was demolished decades ago. The new buyer scrapped his plans to build an apartment block there. Lack of funds. The lot hasn't been leased out since." Matt reviewed his notes again. "Another resident told me he heard that Bill Hardy had relocated to Montreal. He was working part-time in a restaurant called Your Basic Kitchen."

"Did you contact the restaurant?"

"Yes. They didn't recognize his name. No surprise there. The place changed ownership a couple of times. Bill must have moved on years ago." Matt's eyes narrowed. "Wait a minute, Ryan. You're not going to tell me to call every restaurant in town to find him, are you? There are five thousand restaurants in the Greater Montreal Area!"

"You don't have to." He handed him a report. "Cory located Bill's name in the database. A driving violation."

Matt scanned the data. "Is the address current?"

"We don't know. You can check it out tomorrow morning. Amber will go with you."

"Amber?" A frown formed between Matt's eyes.

"Me?" I echoed.

Matt gestured in our direction. "I thought you two worked together."

"We usually do," Ryan said, "but I have a meeting with the homicide team tomorrow."

"Oh." Matt sounded disappointed.

Was it personal? "Matt, do you have a problem going to the interview with me tomorrow?" I asked him.

Matt dismissed my suggestion with a flap of his hand. "No. It's nothing like that. It's just that...well..." He switched his gaze to Ryan. "I miss the guys in homicide. I wish they'd call me up once in a while."

Ryan kept his voice low. "Be careful what you wish for. If we don't solve more cold cases, the lieutenant will transfer both of us back to homicide. Permanently."

"Wow! He actually said that?"

"Not in so many words, but yes." Ryan had a final question for Matt. "Did any other names of interest pop up during your visit to Willowburg?"

"Not so far."

"As for Bill, I suggest you and Amber visit him unannounced tomorrow. He was the last person to speak with Susan at the diner. More than anyone else, he can provide firsthand details about his conversation with her."

"Great idea," Matt said. "Anything new with you guys?"

"Corey found Richard Kendall," I said. "He's living in a long-term care facility in Verdun. We have no idea what his health is like. Ryan and I will visit him this week to interview him."

Matt gave us a thumbs-up. "Looks like we got the ball rolling on this case."

It was late evening before the snowplows cleared the roads. As I had feared, my car wouldn't start. After getting a jump-start with Corey's assistance and jumper cables, I drove home and fell into bed, exhausted from the long day.

But thoughts about Susan Kendall's case and the pressure to solve it prevented me from falling into a deep slumber. If my disturbing emotional reactions to the evidence was any indication of things to come, how would I be able to handle interviews with potential suspects?

Richard Kendall, for one.

A surge of anxiety flowed over me. How would I feel being in the same room as a man who beat his wife and might have killed his own daughter? Would I remain calm enough to carry on a conversation with him? Or would a whirlwind of emotions overwhelm me?

I'd find out soon enough.

8

———

I arrived at the office earlier than usual the next morning and headed straight for the kitchen. I poured myself a cup of coffee in a mug that had my name on it. It was a pre-Christmas gift last week from Lieutenant Payton. Each employee in our division received one with their name inscribed on it. Word circulated that our boss had received a holiday discount and taken advantage of the deal.

Ryan entered the building minutes later and greeted me with a smile. He'd stayed at his place last night, opting for a chance to catch up on laundry. It didn't sound as if he disliked doing that particular task. In fact, he seemed pleased about it. I took note for future reference if I ever agreed to move in with him.

Despite their workload, Corey and Nadia managed to launch the page for Susan Kendall on the police website. It included the birthday photo that Debra had given us and Susan's brief family history, leaving out the alleged violence. Corey added photos of the old diner and neighboring streets from the town's historic records. Our goal was that these details

would jog someone's memory and nudge them to contact us
through the Info-Crime line.

~

Matt and I set out in the afternoon for our interview with Bill
Hardy, former owner of The Easy Diner. It turned out that the
address Corey had given us for him was correct.

At eighty-two years old, Bill hardly exemplified an aging
senior. He had muscular arms, a trim figure, and white bristly
hair cropped short. Looking relaxed in jeans and a T-shirt, he
invited Matt and me to sit down on one of the two sofas in his
living room. He settled in the one across from us.

Bill's rental apartment was neat and sparsely furnished. Gold
trophies and plates from sports events on a single corner table
were credits to his good health and stamina over the past decades.
A tall lamp stood in their midst, as if to keep the spotlight on his
awards when daylight faded. A recent photo of him sitting on a
couch next to a golden retriever completed the collection.

Bill noticed my lingering interest in the awards. "One thing I
learned over the years was how important it is to stay active. It
keeps the body young and strong." He smiled widely, keeping
his eyes on me.

Was he flirting with me?

Matt cleared his throat. "Mr. Hardy, we're here to—"

"Please call me Bill. The mister thing makes me feel so
damn old." He chuckled.

"Bill, we have a few questions about one of your former
employees at the diner in Willowburg. Susan Kendall."

"Your contact person at the unit mentioned her name. I'm
sorry, but I don't remember Susan Kendall. Hundreds of young
people have worked for me at the diner. I can't remember all
their names."

I retrieved Debra's photo from my pocket and showed it to

him. "This is a photo of Susan and another employee, Debra Robinson."

Bill leaned forward on the sofa and peered at the photo. "Debra. I remember her. She dated one of my friends. She was a hard worker." He squinted at the photo, then pulled back. "I don't remember the other girl at all."

"Susan quit her job at your diner on Christmas Eve in 1983," I said. "The day she was killed."

"Like I said, I don't remember her."

Anger rose inside me. "How can you not remember her? Her murder was front-page news in the local paper and included her picture. If anything, you should recall being interviewed by the police about her death. It's something most people don't experience in a lifetime."

Bill's eyes darted around the room as if he were trying to dream up another excuse, but he remained silent.

"Let me jog your memory," I said. "You had an argument with Susan minutes before she quit that day. Witnesses claim it was a heated one."

His expression lit up with recognition. "Oh, yeah, I remember her now, that little troublemaker." He gritted his teeth. "I was furious. I'll never forgive her for walking out on me."

"Were you angry enough to kill her?"

"What are you implying?"

"Susan was murdered shortly after she left the diner."

Bill's lips tightened. "If you're suggesting I killed her, you're dead wrong." He glared at me. "I was mad as hell, though. She quit at the last minute without any warning."

I didn't hold back. "Maybe she quit because you weren't paying her enough."

Bill blinked in surprise. "I don't know where you get your information, but you're mistaken. Young people constantly applied for a job at my diner. In fact, I won an award for being one of the best employers in Willowburg." He raised his chin with pride.

"Our sources confirm that your employees often worked overtime without pay," I persisted.

He tempered his tone. "Look, I felt bad paying them minimum wage, but my diner wasn't a charity. I had a business to run."

His efforts to play on our emotions was a façade. This man was no softy. Something else bothered me and I voiced it. "Most of the girls quit their jobs at the diner after a short period. Why was that?"

He stiffened. "It was only about the money for them. Those young people were constantly asking me for a raise, as if they didn't make enough with tips on top of their salaries." He huffed. "They forced me to sell the diner."

"Forced you?" Matt repeated. "How?"

Bill crossed his arms. "Staff rotation."

Matt didn't buy his excuse. "Really? Why was that?"

"Sergeant, you should know why. A man of your experience."

"Tell me."

"I guess you don't know much after all," Bill snickered, mocking him. "There were better job prospects in big cities. What else?" He blinked rapidly, a sign he was lying.

Matt smiled tightly and kept it professional. "You said you sold your diner."

"That's right. I sold it to an interested buyer and invested the money. No one can afford to live on the crappy old age pension the government gives us."

"Did you work afterward?"

"Yes. At other diners in the area. Part-time mainly."

"Like where exactly?" Matt asked.

"Small towns near here that you've probably never heard of," Bill snapped.

"Try me."

"Cedarberry, for one. I can't recall the names of the others." Bill glanced at a clock on the wall. "Any other questions?"

"Let's go back to Susan Kendall," I said. "Witnesses told us she quit her job on Christmas Eve. The diner must have been a busy place that evening."

"What do you think?" Bill squinted in annoyance. "Every Christmas Eve is busy. I'm sure we were scrambling in the kitchen like crazy, clearing tables, taking orders from customers..." He briefly glanced away. "I remember I had to send my assistant cook out for extra supplies because we were running out."

How odd that he recalled that tiny detail but not Susan's death. Did he have a selective memory problem? I doubted it.

Bill's irate mood was meant to deter me from asking more questions. But I stayed strong and played my last card. I blurted, "Did you know Susan was pregnant?"

"Pregnant? No. How the hell would I know that?" He raised his arms in the air, then let then fall to his thighs with a firm thud. "Do you think my employees talked to me about their private lives?"

"Several witnesses claim you came on to Susan," Matt said, exaggerating the number.

"Don't try to pin that one on me," Bill sneered, pointing a forefinger at him. "I never touched the girl."

An image of a furious Bill waving a fist in the air appeared before me. I slid a hand into my pocket and clasped the amethyst crystal. Serenity instantly flowed over me.

In the next moment, we witnessed another mood swing. Bill calmed down and rested an arm on the back of the couch. "You might want to talk to Devon Hill, though. He worked as an assistant cook for me back then. He was kind of sweet on the girl. You know what I mean?" He twisted his lips in a grin.

Matt ignored the blatant insinuation and took note of Devon's name. "What can you tell us about Devon?"

"He was a very good cook but a lousy cleaner in the kitchen.

I liked my pots and pans to shine, but he was sloppy. He'd leave water spots on them. Aside from that, he was a nervous guy. He took a lot of smoke breaks, compared with me and the rest of my staff. I didn't say anything because he was a hard worker."

A dog's bark sounded from an adjoining room.

Bill pointed a thumb over his shoulder. "That's Daisy, my golden retriever. I take her out for a walk a few times a day. It's like clockwork for her. She's due now."

"We'll be going." Matt stood up. "Thanks for your time, Mr. Hardy."

Matt's return to using the formality of his name wasn't lost on Bill. He scowled before he led us toward the door, no doubt relieved to close it firmly behind us.

9

On our way back to the car, Matt asked me, "What's your gut feeling about Bill Hardy?" He eyed me with curiosity.

"I'm not sure," I said.

"Why not?"

"Bill lied to us about his connection with Susan. He was furious when she quit, but I'm not sure he killed her."

"I thought you sensed these things more clearly."

"Sometimes. Not always right away."

Cynicism flickered in Matt's eyes. It wasn't the first time I'd seen that hint of doubt. Ryan had the same reaction when we started working on cases together. He gradually got used to the way I deciphered the insights I gathered.

Like I did with Ryan, I explained to Matt how I can't provide the information he was anticipating at the snap of a finger. "The interpretation of what I perceive often comes to me later and when I least expect it."

"Weird," Matt said, grimacing. "Better late than never, I suppose."

After we returned to the unit, we joined Ryan in the conference room. A couple of files and two bankers boxes on the table stirred my curiosity. More cold cases for us?

From the ten chairs around the expansive oval table, Matt and I chose seats opposite Ryan. He listened while Matt and I related the highlights of our visit with Bill Hardy.

Matt mentioned Bill's mood swings. "I swear, Ryan, it's like we were talking to Dr. Jekyll and Mr. Hyde. He was furious one minute and calm the next."

"He said staff rotation was the reason he had to sell the diner," I said. "Can you imagine the nerve?"

Ryan smiled and sat back in his chair. "Sounds like he was playing games with you two. His reputation in that town must have suffered with all those young people quitting on him over time."

"The sole reason the girls quit their jobs was because Bill came on to them," Matt said.

I wasn't done venting my irritation. "On top of everything, Bill claimed he didn't remember Susan Kendall. Who doesn't remember when one of your employees gets killed? And he didn't even show compassion for her death."

"When Susan left her job at the last minute," Matt said, "it must have pushed Bill over the edge. I'd bet he snapped and killed her."

Ryan leaned forward. "I agree that Susan could have provoked built-up anger in him. Genuine hatred caused her violent death. The tough part is proving it was Bill's motive for killing her."

I drew on the image I'd perceived of Bill when we were interviewing him. "His argument with Susan that last day was about something more serious than her quitting her job."

Matt gawked at me. "Where did that come from?"

"Call it a delayed reaction to my insight about him."

"That's how it works for Amber," Ryan said. "Sometimes she needs a little break to interpret an impression after she perceives it."

Matt gave me a thumbs-up. "Like I said earlier, better late than never."

"Since Bill is a plausible suspect," Ryan said, "we'll keep him on the list. Let's get Corey to check out Devon Hill, the assistant cook. He could turn out to be a useful lead."

I pointed to the two bankers boxes and folders. "New cases?"

Ryan tapped one of the evidence boxes. "I might have a new lead on Susan Kendall's case."

"That's encouraging news," Matt said. "Did a witness come forward?"

"No," Ryan said. "On a hunch, I searched the database for similar murders."

I reminded him, "Didn't you say there were no other homicides within a specific perimeter of Susan's murder, like twenty miles?"

"At the time, yes," he said. "But since Corey and Nadia have uploaded lots more cold case files from storage, the database gave me an easier option for an extended search to twenty-five miles. There might be more murders, but I found two other cases with similar circumstances as Susan's."

My heart pounded. "How similar?"

Ryan tapped the folders. "Two other women were killed within the same time frame as Susan, give or take a few weeks. The point of interest is the evidence. To begin with, both victims were stabbed."

"Lots of victims are stabbed," Matt said.

"Ryan, there must be more to these cases if you flagged them," I said.

"There is," he said. "I haven't reviewed all the details, but the evidence left at each crime scene includes three burnt matches."

His discovery astounded me. "That's not a coincidence. These murders have to be the work of a serial killer."

Ryan nodded in agreement. "It's the most logical deduction."

"But the other day, you told me Susan's murderer wasn't a serial killer."

"I also said these guys are unpredictable, and they don't always stick to the rules."

I wasn't sure whether or not to be comforted by this abrupt change in theory. "Looking for a serial killer can make these three cases even more challenging now."

"The matches are the perp's calling cards," Ryan said. "They serve as his signature. He's staking his claim on these victims by leaving burnt matches behind." He slid the files across the table to Matt. "I'd like you to investigate these two murders."

Matt flipped opened the files and read the names. "Michelle Roy, twenty years old, former resident of Trimville. Pamela Cooper, twenty-one years old, former resident of Cedarberry." He asked Ryan, "Are there any suspects?"

"Not yet," Ryan said.

"What should I be looking for?"

"This is my take on a profiler analysis. Seeing as the murders occurred a certain number of miles apart, my theory is that the perp traveled as part of his job. It leads me to assume he functioned outside his comfort zone. Not like your typical serial killer who usually limits himself to an area close to his own home."

"What's in those evidence boxes?" Matt gestured toward them.

"That's where Amber comes in," Ryan said. "Amber, do you feel comfortable trying to get impressions from the evidence right now?"

"I'll give it a try." From Michelle Roy's evidence box, I pulled out the transparent bag containing three matches. The outline of a man came charging at me. I gasped and dropped the bag.

"What did you see?" Ryan asked.

"A very angry man. I can't make out his features, though."

"Was it the same man from the evidence in Susan Kendall's case?"

"I'm not sure."

"That's okay. Try the next one."

I retrieved the evidence bag that held three burnt matches connected to Pamela Cooper's case. The same image of a furious man sprang before me, this time with a knife. I caught my breath. "The same man killed both of these women."

"Then we're undeniably looking for a perp who's a serial killer," Ryan said.

His encouraging comment boosted my confidence and reinforced the fact that I should trust my insights more often. "These two perceptions have a common feature: a man with the same intense anger and surge of movement. I'm now positive that this man killed Susan Kendall too."

"That's wild!" Matt leaned forward with interest. "Ryan, when do I start interviewing witnesses?"

"ASAP," Ryan said. "Solving these three cases would be a bonus for us. There's nothing like the lieutenant threatening to terminate the unit if we don't meet our quota. Right?"

Matt and I groaned in agreement.

Ryan went on. "Matt, start by tracking down the witnesses. Gather everything you can find on them and copy me. Corey or Nadia can help you with the search. Then interview as many people as you can in person."

Matt stood up. "I'm on it."

"I'll send the three sets of matches to forensics for testing," Ryan said, his tone upbeat. "It could take a week or so, but it's worth the wait. They might come up with fingerprints or DNA that can help us track down Susan's killer."

I shared Ryan's optimism that things were finally moving. All the more reason that I was eager to interview our next witness.

10

It was early afternoon when Ryan and I set out for our interview with Dr. Kenneth Cameron. Seeing as Susan Kendall and Kenneth had enjoyed a close relationship, meeting him in person would give me a chance to obtain valuable impressions.

Forensics had processed Susan's ultrasound photo for fingerprints but had found no matches in the criminal database. Since Ryan and I needed to find out if Kenneth knew about Susan's pregnancy, we planned to show him the photo and test his reaction to it. His response could determine if the pregnancy had stood in the way of advancing his medical career or discrediting his family's reputation. Whatever the reason, it could provide a motive for murder.

I tucked the evidence envelope containing the photo into my pocket. The element of surprise was on our side. I planned to take in every word, action, and feeling that the doctor might reveal when faced with a piece of his past.

As I slid into the passenger seat of the unmarked police car, Ryan said, "I missed you." He reached for my hand and squeezed it.

I squeezed back. "Me too." I glanced around in case someone might have seen us. Then again, no one could have spotted our romantic gesture behind the tinted glass windows of our police car.

Twenty minutes later, we were sitting in Dr. Kenneth Cameron's downtown office, waiting for him to arrive. An ornate wood desk that looked as if he'd inherited it decades ago took up half the floor space. On a bookcase behind him, photos of a younger Kenneth with his parents were outnumbered by subsequent photos taken with his wife, children, and grandchildren. Photos of two dogs and a cat were included.

A side door opened. Kenneth dashed in and introduced himself. Now sixty-four years old, he'd retained his boyish features and trim figure. From his handshake, I perceived a high energy level.

A slight odor of cigarette smoke filled the air. Was I imagining it? I focused on the pockets of Kenneth's white lab coat for signs of a pack of cigarettes or a lighter but saw none.

Kenneth sat down in a maroon leather chair across the desk from us. "What can I do for you?"

Ryan introduced the topic. "As you know, doctor, we've reopened Susan Kendall's case. Sources tell us that you dated her."

"Sergeant, you take me back decades," Kenneth said, smiling briefly. "Susan was a sweet young girl who worked at a diner in Willowburg. What was the name? Oh, yes. The Easy Diner."

"We were told that your relationship was serious and that you planned to get married."

"Well..." Kenneth hesitated. "She was a teenager, and I was working through medical school as an intern. Marriage would have been highly unlikely at the time."

"But you did have plans to marry her, right?" Ryan prompted him.

"Yes, but later." Kenneth straightened a notebook on his desk. "We were going to live together first."

I sensed that the doctor was holding something back. "Can you tell us what you remember about the last day you saw Susan?" I asked him.

"The last day..." Kenneth's eyes wandered around the room as he dredged up the memory. "Actually, I didn't see her. The next day, I found out she was murdered. I was horrified."

"We understand you were planning to leave town with Susan after work that day," I said.

"Yes. We were supposed to meet after her shift ended."

"Where?"

"In front of a flower shop in town. I'd planned to get there before closing at five o'clock and buy her a bouquet of flowers, but I was late. I had to work an extended shift at the hospital."

"An extended shift?"

"Several hours more."

"Did you try to reach Susan to tell her?"

"I called the diner from the hospital, but she'd already left," Kenneth said with a shrug. "I assumed she'd gone to the apartment she shared with another employee, so I went there after work. No one was home."

"What did you do then?" I asked him.

"I went back to our meeting place in front of the flower shop. Most of the stores had closed by then since it was Christmas Eve. It was snowing hard and fast, so I went into a coffee shop nearby in case she was there. She wasn't."

"Where did you go afterward?"

"As crazy as it sounds," Kenneth said as if to excuse his behavior, "I drove to her father's house outside town. Susan had told me how cruel he was. I was afraid something had gone terribly wrong. When I knocked at the door, her father opened it. He smelled of alcohol and looked grubby, as if he hadn't washed in days. After I identified myself, he grabbed an ax and threatened me. He warned me never to come to the house again and slammed the door on me."

His revelation astounded me. "What did you do?"

"I drove back to town. The roads were awful. A blizzard had dropped more than a foot of snow. The wind had caused high drifts everywhere. I thought I was going to get stuck, but I made it back. On impulse, I drove to the flower shop." He paused, frowning. "I got out of the car and looked around, wondering where Susan could have gone. I walked toward the flower shop and stopped. All I saw were garbage bags covered with snow in the alley next to it. I was about to leave when I heard someone call my name. I waited, but I didn't hear it again. I assumed it was the howling wind or my mind playing tricks on me. I'd worked sixteen hours straight that day."

"What did you do afterward?"

"I went back to her apartment, but again, no one was home. I returned to the coffee shop. It was the only place still open." He looked away, as if remembering. "Funny thing, a few carolers were there. They were singing 'Silent Night.' Ironic, isn't it?" He shook his head.

"They found Susan in the alley near the flower shop the next morning," I said, unable to hide the bitterness in my voice.

"I know." He blinked hard as if to wipe the memory away. "I regret to this day that I didn't venture further into that alley. I could have found her before it was too late."

Was he sincere? It was hard to tell.

I pulled out the evidence bag containing the ultrasound photo of Susan's baby and showed it to him. "Does this picture mean anything to you?"

Kenneth peered at it. "It's an ultrasound image of a fetus."

"Do you know who the mother is?"

"No." He stared at me. "Should I?"

"It's Susan's baby. Did you know she was pregnant?"

His brow wrinkled in surprise. "What?"

"She was about three months pregnant," I said.

Kenneth shook his head in denial. "It's impossible. I understand that these things do happen, but we took precautions. Aside from that, Susan would have told me if she was pregnant."

It was a logical deduction. Why would Susan keep her pregnancy a secret from him? What was she hiding?

"The autopsy report confirmed Susan's pregnancy," I said. "Since you were about to marry her, why wouldn't she have told you or shown you the photo?"

Sadness crossed Kenneth's face. He lowered his head. "I have no answer for that. Her pregnancy comes as a complete revelation to me."

His words rang empty somehow—unless someone else was the father.

Ryan stepped in. "Did your parents approve of your relationship with Susan?"

Kenneth held up a hand in protest. "My parents had nothing to do with the women I dated. I was twenty-one, old enough to make my own decisions."

"Which decisions were those?"

"I told you. We planned to leave town...find an apartment...get married later." He glanced away, as if he were recalling a memory. "Susan was a wonderful person. She didn't deserve to die like that."

Was Kenneth truly saddened by her death? What if a pregnant Susan meant he'd have to put his dream of becoming a doctor on hold? Did he get rid of her so that her pregnancy didn't ruin his career plans?

I was determined to find out. "A baby on the way and a future marriage. Wouldn't that situation have put a strain on your career plans?"

Kenneth glowered. "If you're referring to my financial situation, no. I was quite capable of meeting my obligations."

That much was true. According to Debra, his family had provided him with a trust fund by age twenty-one. And yet...

"Your parents sponsored numerous charity events in the area," I said. "What about your family reputation? You were fathering a child out of wedlock."

He squirmed slightly in his chair. "Like I said, we were planning to leave town. Since no one knew about the pregnancy, including me, it wouldn't have mattered, would it?"

Kenneth's claim conflicted with Debra's testimony about his parents and their elite perspective on life, specifically, they would discourage the rich-boy-marries-poor-girl dilemma. Whom should we believe?

Ryan picked up the conversation. "Doctor, did you attend medical school after Susan died?"

"Not right away," Kenneth said. "My father wanted me to join his company and help promote the family strawberry business. It was their dream."

"In the winter?"

"They sold fresh and frozen fruit throughout the year."

"How long did you work for your father?"

"Not long. January to February. I was on the road a lot, visiting small-town merchants to big-city grocery chains. I left in the spring to pursue a medical career."

The photo of a smiling family of five sat on the bookcase behind him. "You got married and raised three children," I said.

Kenneth smiled. "Yes. My wife and I are very proud of them."

His alleged unawareness of Susan's pregnancy continued to trouble me. "Speaking of children, I have a question about Susan's pregnancy. What if it wasn't your baby she was carrying?"

Kenneth's forehead crinkled. "Susan was faithful to me. That much I was certain of."

His reply was vague. Something wasn't quite right. Either Kenneth was lying to us, or he'd been tricked into believing that the unborn baby was his and didn't want to admit he knew about the pregnancy.

Ryan indicated he shared my suspicions when he said, "Doctor, we'd like you to provide us with a sample of your DNA and fingerprints."

"I'd be glad to," Kenneth said.

As soon as we returned to the unit, Ryan arranged with a forensic team to collect the samples. It would take at least a week before results came back from the lab.

I could hardly wait.

11

———

The next day, Nadia dug up details about the high school that Susan Kendall had attended. She also found an old photo of the school that she uploaded to Susan's page on the police website.

"Our Lady of Fatima," Nadia said to Ryan and me. "It was the only high school in the area. The building was sold and converted into an apartment block decades ago."

"Were you able to locate any former contacts with the school?" Ryan asked.

"Yes." Nadia's glossy pink smile stretched across her pale complexion as she fingered two sheets of paper. "We have Paul Barnett, the principal of the school, and Jennifer Sarto, a former schoolteacher." She handed him the reports. "I set up your meetings with them for tomorrow afternoon."

"Good work," Ryan said.

"Thanks." Nadia strutted off.

"I doubt we can access student school records from that far back," I said to Ryan. "If they exist, that is."

"Maybe these two new witnesses will remember Susan," he

said, "especially if they were aware she had a history of family violence."

As if fate had been listening to our conversation, the Info-Crime line produced a surprise caller in the afternoon. Nadia transferred the call to Ryan, but he determined that I should take it to try to get a reading over the phone.

I accessed the line and introduced myself. "You're calling about the website video on Susan Kendall?"

"Yes, thank you for reopening the case," the female caller said. "I'm her sister, Lisa."

The image of a little girl and a slightly older one whizzed before me. "I'm so sorry for your loss, Lisa. What would you like to tell me?"

"I miss my older sister."

No words could lessen her pain. It tugged at my heart-strings, and I fought to keep my concentration on the questions I wanted to ask her. "Lisa, can you tell me anything that could help the police find your sister's killer?"

"I can tell you this much. I wouldn't be surprised if my father killed Susan."

My heart pumped faster. "That's a strong statement. Can you back it up?"

"He was a violent man. If my mother or sister disobeyed him in the slightest way, he struck out at them. I hated him so much. I still do." Her voice quavered. "I'll probably regret saying this one day, but if he isn't on your list of suspects, he should be."

A meeting with her would enhance my ability to tap into the truth. "Lisa, can Sergeant Detective Baxter and I meet with you?"

"Not today. My shift at the hospital starts in an hour."

I didn't want her to hang up just yet. "Do you know where your father is now?"

"He's in a long-term care facility called Starlight Homes. I arranged to place him there after he got a stroke and was living alone in a filthy rental room."

"A stroke? When?"

"It happened several years after I left Willowburg. I was working and supporting myself. He went into a rage the day I told him he couldn't stay with me in my apartment instead. He's had it out for me since then."

"Lisa, did your father ever harm you physically?" I asked.

"No. I suppose I should be grateful for that. Sometimes I wish he had, instead of watching him beat my mother to death."

Her implication stunned me. "Are you saying that—"

"No, he didn't kill her. After all the times he hit her, I'm surprised she lived so long."

I needed eyewitness confirmation. "How did your mother die?"

Lisa huffed. "They told me she fell down the stairs and broke her neck. I was at school, but I..." She stopped. "I have to go to work now."

"Would you prefer to come to our office to meet with us?"

"It might be risky."

"Risky? How?"

Lisa drew a breath and exhaled. "The truth is I'm scared."

"Of what?"

"Of him."

"Why?"

She didn't answer.

I changed the subject. "Lisa, I'd like to keep in touch," I said softly. "Can you give me your address and cell number?"

She gave me the information.

"If you remember anything else that could help us solve Susan's murder," I said as a final plea, "please contact the hotline and ask to speak with me."

"Okay." She ended the call.

Lisa's revelation raised my suspicion about her father to a

new level. He was an older man today, but his age didn't cancel the harm he could have inflicted decades ago.

After Ryan listened to the recorded conversation, I said to him, "If this doesn't add doubts about Richard Kendall's innocence, what does?"

"We can't eliminate him, that's for sure," he said. "I'll ask Corey to set up an interview with him ASAP."

To our surprise, Richard Kendall agreed to meet with us at Starlight Homes this same day. I mentally reviewed the questions I'd ask him. How would he react to the alleged accusations against him, from wife beatings to murder? Would he deny them? Would he feign memory loss?

Ryan slipped into his jacket. "It's time we find out exactly what Richard Kendall has to say about all this. Let's go visit the man."

12

____

A dull sky hovered on our drive to Starlight Homes, a long-term care facility south of the city core. It was an indication that more snow was on the way. Snowplows had cleared the main streets but left the bordering snowbanks. The placement of sporadic No Parking signs indicated that snow crews were scheduled to remove the mounds during the next twenty-four hours.

To our relief, the parking area for visitors behind Starlight Homes had been cleared of snow. A semicircle of trees isolated the facility from the neighboring residential district and gave one a sense of comfort and security.

After Ryan signed in for us at the front desk, we waited to be escorted to Richard Kendall's room. The odor inside the building smelled like an air freshener with a floral scent. The floors were clean and polished, and in-ceiling lights brightened the lobby.

An attendant arrived and accompanied us to Richard Kendall's room, her shoes tapping softly along the linoleum floor. I braced myself for what I anticipated would be a stressful meeting with a potential criminal.

Richard sat in a wheelchair. His head was slightly tilted to one side. He was much thinner than I'd imagined. He was bony and clad in a navy bathrobe over plaid flannel pajamas. Parkinson's disease had debilitated him, causing tremors in both hands. He wasn't the same young man who'd worked long days in construction and shared his muscle power to keep his family in line. This was a man who was vulnerable and unable to care for himself.

Richard's beady eyes narrowed and rested on Ryan and me as if he were sizing us up. He grunted when the attendant explained who we were. She remained by his side as we took our seats, then left and shut the door behind her.

My gaze slid around the room. A small fridge was tucked in a corner. A TV hung on the wall opposite a simple wood bed. A lamp, an envelope, and an old cigarette case topped a night table. An armchair by the window supported a folded blanket on one armrest. There were no framed photos or other signs of family ties in the room.

Uneasiness filled the air. It had nothing to do with the uncontrollable trembling of Richard's hands. It was as if my awareness of his abusive history had opened a door, one that captured the wave of evil emanating from the man.

I tried to remain neutral and read more into my insights but failed. My apprehension was blocking me from capturing any perceptions from the man.

Ryan began. "Mr. Kendall, can you tell us about your relationship with your family?"

"I don't have a family anymore," Richard said, his voice raspy.

Ryan ignored his comment. "Witnesses have stated that the relationship with your wife and daughters were... How shall I put it? Stormy."

"Stormy?" he repeated." What are you talking about?"

"You physically abused your wife and Susan, your daughter."

Richard let out a croaky laugh. "You got proof?"

Ryan didn't hold back. "Where were you the night Susan was murdered?"

Richard raised a shaky hand in the air. "Not that question again. I talked to the cops years ago. Why are you bringing this up now?"

"We reopened the cold case."

"Ha! Good luck with that!"

It wasn't the reply we wanted.

Ryan rephrased his question. "Did you leave the house the night Susan was killed?"

Richard pressed his lips in annoyance.

Ryan waited—his tactic to extract more information.

After a brief silence, Richard said, "Look, I was home all night after a hard day working on a construction project out of town. If you're trying to say I had something to do with Susan's murder, pick someone else to blame."

"You had a visitor that night. A young man. Do you remember?"

"Yeah. Susan's so-called boyfriend."

"What time did he arrive?"

"It was late." Anger flashed in Richard's eyes. "Don't you cops have records of this stuff? I'm sure I answered that question before."

Ryan went on. "Do you keep in touch with Lisa, your other daughter?"

"I knew you'd ask me about her eventually," he grumbled. "The last time she wrote to me was decades ago. Her criticism of me was hurtful, but I kept the letter. Over the years, I saw the man I used to be and lived to regret it. The letter is on the table over there." He motioned with his head. "You can keep it. I don't need it anymore."

I made a move to stand up, but Ryan hurried over to get it. He pulled out a pair of vinyl gloves and a transparent evidence bag from his jacket. He slid the envelope into the bag, then tucked the bag in his pocket. After he sat back down, he asked, "Do you smoke, Mr. Kendall?"

"Why?"

"I noticed the vintage cigarette case on the table."

"It was a gift from my wife. I quit smoking years ago."

I couldn't wait to ask him about his daughter. "Did you know that Susan was pregnant when she was killed?"

Richard grimaced. "Damn right I knew!"

"Did Susan tell you?"

"It's not important. The fact is, I was mad as hell. Excuse the language. It wasn't the way I brought up my girls."

"What do you mean?"

"I made sure that everyone in my family was an honest, devout person who abided by the rules of the house."

I pictured him standing at a church pulpit, preaching to the congregation about fire and damnation. "What rules were those?"

"My rules." Richard's lips formed a tight, straight line.

An image of him slapping a woman in the face sped through my mind. I struggled to contain my resentment. "And if they didn't follow your rules, you beat them and left them with bruises, didn't you?"

Beside me, Ryan fidgeted, a sign he was uneasy with my question.

Between clenched teeth, Richard said, "Young lady, if you weren't law enforcement..." He tried to point a finger at me, but his hand jerked out of control. "Both of you, get out! I'm done with you."

Ryan stood up and left his business card on the bed. "Feel free to call us if you think of anything that would help us with this case."

"Call you?" Richard sniggered. "Do you see a phone in this room? Even if I had one, I can't use it with these hands, nor would I want to."

"Thank you for your time, Mr. Kendall." Ryan led the way out.

A heavy snowfall greeted us as we stepped outdoors. Gusty winds swept large snowflakes into the air and prevented us from seeing more than several feet ahead of us.

Ryan shouted into the wind, "That was quite a daring remark on your part, suggesting that Richard beat the women in his family."

"It was the truth," I said.

"Did you get any insights during the interview?"

"Yes. I saw Richard hitting a woman."

"Can you describe her?"

"No. Sorry."

"Don't be sorry. You're giving it your best shot."

Leave it to Ryan to give me a boost even when I failed at something. No wonder I loved him!

"The image you saw," he said. "It could be his wife or Susan. If Richard knew that Susan was pregnant, word of such a scandal in a small town would have spread fast and damaged his reputation. What was left of it."

A blast of wind blew snow into my face, blinding me. "Ugh!" I stopped in my tracks.

"Here." Ryan linked his arm in mine. "Damaging Richard's reputation is nothing when you compare how angry he must have been when Susan's pregnancy broke all his rules," he said with a touch of sarcasm.

"I agree, but he lost control over her when she moved out. She was an adult." My thoughts strayed. "As far as motive goes, I'm not sure that Richard's public disgrace would have been reason enough to kill Susan."

"People have killed for lesser reasons. Ask yourself this question: What if he turns out to be our prime suspect?"

Ryan's irony wasn't lost on me. Often motivated by hatred, jealousy, or revenge, domestic violence was nothing new. "Maybe Lisa can enlighten us."

"We'll read her letter in the car."

Our coats were covered with layers of snow. They quickly evaporated after we stepped inside the car and Ryan turned on the heater. He went back outside to brush the snow off the car.

I watched as he meticulously swept the windshield, then the side windows. He stopped and smiled at me, and I smiled back. How lucky I was to have such a caring man in my life, not to mention a brilliant investigative partner!

After Ryan settled in the driver's seat, he pulled out a pair of vinyl gloves and retrieved the transparent evidence bag containing Lisa's letter from his pocket. Without removing the envelope, he examined it. "There's no return address. Good thing she gave it to you when she called the Info-Crime line. We'll have to schedule a visit with her."

"She didn't sound as if she was eager to meet with us," I said.

"She's next of kin. She might not have a choice." He removed Lisa's letter from the envelope and read it out loud.

Dad, this will be the last time I write to you. You don't deserve to be my father. I hate what you did to Mom and the awful way you treated Susan and me. I want nothing more to do with you. Lisa

"At least Richard told us he regretted the way he lived his past," I said.

"He was a different man back then." Ryan steered the car out of the parking lot and onto the street. "Is he a cold-blooded killer? That's for us to find out. We'll keep him on our list of potential suspects for now."

Bill Hardy, Kenneth Cameron, and now Richard Kendall. With no solid evidence to incriminate any of them, our investigation was firmly stuck in limbo.

13

Matt arrived at the unit after lunch with a bleak statement about his witness interviews. "My first round didn't go as planned." He deposited a large cup of coffee on his desk.

I swiveled my chair to face him. "What happened?"

Ryan got up from his desk and joined us. "What's up, Matt?"

Matt sank his plump frame into his chair, creating a creaking noise. "I had six witnesses lined up in the Michelle Roy case, and four of them are deceased," he said, disappointment in his voice.

"And the other two?" Ryan asked.

"Oh, you're going to love this." Matt's demeanor brightened. "I hit pay dirt with witness number five. The guy was a teenager at the time. He was working the night shift as a busser at a fast-food restaurant in Trimville when he found the body of Michelle Roy. Trimville is about twenty-five miles from Willowburg."

"What's the guy's name?"

"Devon Hill."

Devon Hill. A familiar name. "He was working at Bill Hardy's diner when Susan Kendall was killed," I said.

"Oh, hell!" Matt did a facepalm in embarrassment. "That's where I heard that name before."

"Did Devon mention he'd worked at The Easy Diner in Willowburg?" I asked him. "That he knew Susan Kendall?"

"No," Matt said. "I guess it slipped his mind, seeing as we were discussing a different victim."

It had evidently slipped Matt's mind as well.

Lines across Ryan's forehead showed his displeasure with Matt's oversight, but he held back from reproaching him. "What's your reading of the guy?"

Matt shrugged. "I don't know. I interviewed him on the phone."

"On the phone. Why not in person?"

"He refused to meet with me. He claimed it was too dangerous."

"Too dangerous? How?"

"He didn't say."

Matt was cutting corners. It wasn't the first time he'd circumvented the legwork part of an investigation.

The lines in Ryan's forehead deepened. "What else did Devon tell you?"

Matt reviewed the notes on his phone. "It was a busy night around New Year's. He'd taken out the garbage and noticed a pile behind the restaurant that hadn't been there earlier. He thought a drunk had chosen that spot and fallen asleep. Or a drifter. They sometimes pass through Trimville on their way to a big city."

"We're talking days after Susan Kendall was murdered, right?"

"Right." Matt continued. "Anyway, there was a blizzard, so the garbage pile out back was partly covered with snow. Devon brushed some of it off. He freaked out when he realized it was a dead woman staring up at him. He scrambled inside to tell the owner of the restaurant. The owner called the cops."

"The circumstances and evidence in Michelle Roy's case are similar to Susan's case," Ryan said.

"No kidding. We could be looking at the same perp."

"That's what we intend to find out," Ryan said. "You need to interview Devon in person. Ask him why he quit his job at The Easy Diner. He might provide a lead of sorts."

"I'm on it."

"And your last witness, Matt?"

"My number six witness was a woman in Cedarberry named Catherine Lambert. It's about twenty-two miles from Willowburg. Population of about five thousand. She worked at a clothing store and discovered the body of Pamela Cooper behind the place. Pamela was murdered a couple of weeks after the other two victims."

"When will you be interviewing this witness?"

"Tomorrow."

"In person?"

"Yes."

Ryan summed up our three cold cases. "Okay. We have three young female victims stabbed and left in the snow near businesses. Three burnt matches were left at each scene. In essence, we have the same MOs for all our victims."

"When Amber did her thing with the evidence, she saw the same perp in all three cases," Matt reminded him.

"There you go." Ryan threw a subtle look of admiration in my direction. "I don't want to get ahead of the analysis we're expecting from forensics regarding the matches. Let me say that, if there's a connection linking these three stabbings, it means we're getting closer to finding the killer. Hypothetically, the same killer of all three victims."

Encouragement ran through Ryan's voice.

I wished I felt the same way. Something was bothering me, and I couldn't explain it.

14

In the afternoon, Ryan and I had interviews scheduled with two people who'd worked at the high school Susan Randall had attended. These witnesses might have had interactions with the teenage Susan that would reveal more about her turbulent family life.

Former school principal Paul Barnett lived in a section of Old Montreal where streets had recently been converted to pedestrian-only traffic. With snow removal crews restricting street parking in the area, we had to drive two blocks farther to find indoor parking, then walk back to our destination.

A balding man with a short gray beard welcomed us into his apartment. "Please call me Paul," he said after Ryan had addressed him as Mr. Barnett. "I've heard enough 'mister' all my life." He chuckled, then led us into the living room.

A soaring bookcase lined half of the farthest wall and displayed hundreds of books. A quick glance told me Paul enjoyed reading the classics, historical fiction, and travel literature. Framed photos and tiny figurines dotted the few empty spaces on stuffed shelves.

Ryan and I sat in the sofa adjacent to the bulky armchair

that Paul occupied. Although I questioned the formality of Paul's attire—a jacket over a shirt and bow tie—he appeared relaxed.

Ryan began. "Paul, as our contact person informed you, we've reopened Susan Kendall's case. We're looking for information that could lead us to her killer."

"That's a tall order. How can I help you?"

"Tell us about Susan as a student."

"Ah, yes. When your police contact called to set up this meeting, Susan Kendall's name wasn't familiar to me. To help me out, I requested a search at the school board. I'm retired, but I have connections in the archives department." He winked. "Records indicate that Susan was an average student. There were no major problems reported."

"Major problems?" Ryan repeated. "Can you give me examples?"

"Frequent absences from school, class disturbances, trouble with the law...things like that. In fact, those were rare occurrences in the eighties. It was a much quieter period back then than it is today."

"Were any family problems recorded in Susan's file?" I asked him.

"No," he said. "To be honest, I had limited contact with the students. Susan had a closer relationship with her teachers. They could assist you more in that area."

Since the former school principal had nothing more to say, we thanked him and left.

"I doubt students were that different in the eighties," I said to Ryan as we returned to the car. "Kids broke the rules and got into trouble, no matter what decade."

"Sometimes the school admins held back from notifying the authorities," he said. "A black mark on their records damaged the school's reputation. Of course, it's a far cry from what's happening in today's schools. Crime has increased and is sensationalized through media coverage, which can influence copycats."

"Speaking of media, it has a positive side. There's always a chance that our website page on Susan Kendall could trigger a call that would lead to her killer."

Ryan shrugged. "I'd call that wishful thinking. On the other hand, it would be one lucky break if it did happen."

Our second meeting was with Jennifer Sarto, a former schoolteacher who lived in a condominium in the east end of the city. Since teachers have daily contact with their students during the school year, Ryan and I were confident that this interview would provide more personal details about Susan.

The slender woman with the melodic voice invited us to sit at her kitchen table in her open-concept apartment. "I was heartbroken when I heard about Susan's death," she said softly as she poured coffee into our cups. "She was such a sweet girl."

"What can you tell us about her performance in school?" I asked her.

"Well, she loved mathematics but had difficulty with English literature."

"English lit?" It had been one of my favorite subjects.

"It wasn't as if Susan didn't understand the material," Jennifer said. "Her interpretation of classic poetry was excellent. The longer reading material was her problem. When I asked why she hadn't read the stories assigned as part of her homework, she'd say she hadn't had the time to read them."

"What about sports?" Ryan asked her. "Any after-school activities?"

Jennifer shook her head. "She didn't join any of the teams because she couldn't stay after school. Family obligations, she'd tell me whenever I asked."

"Did she specify what obligations?" I asked her.

"No, but I discovered by chance that she worked part-time at the local post office. I happened to go there one day. It was after her mother had passed away. Mrs. Kendall's accident was so untimely for Susan and her sister. They were so young."

"You seem to be quite familiar with Susan's personal life," I said.

Jennifer smiled. "I kept little notes on all my students. I knew that one day, after I retired, I'd have fond memories of them to fall back on. In fact, I took group and individual photos of my graduating students. I was so proud of them."

I seized the opportunity. "Do you have any photos of Susan?"

"Yes, I do." She stood up. "I'll be right back." She entered an adjoining room and returned moments later with a photo of Susan and her friends in their graduating class.

I studied the photo. Dressed in caps and gowns, five girls stood arm in arm and smiled proudly. Susan's cheery expression hid any sign of the turbulence happening at home. "Did Susan ever mention she had family problems?"

"Not really. She was very private."

"How was her health?"

"Fine." Jennifer paused. "On some mornings, though, her eyes were bloodshot, as if she hadn't slept all night. It didn't interfere with her classroom work, so I didn't say anything."

I took it a step further. "Did you ever notice any signs of...injury? Bruises?"

She placed a hand over her heart. "My goodness! Now that you mention it, she did come to class one day with a bumpy bruise on her forehead."

"Did you ask her about it?"

"Of course." Jennifer pressed her lips together. "I was very concerned. She told me she had fallen over a pile of books by her bed and hit the bedpost. She explained how she was accident prone and showed me a couple of bruises on her arms."

"And you didn't suspect she'd been beaten?"

"By whom?"

"We were hoping you could tell us."

"Well, I..." Jennifer's eyelids fluttered nervously. "Rumors were circulating that her father had a violent temper and took it out on his family."

"Yet you or no one in the school administration considered asking child services to investigate?"

"Unfortunately, there were few laws and policies like today to address any complaints." She stared at me, the reality of my allegation finally connecting. "Are you implying that Susan's father had physically abused her?"

A likely guess.

15

The snowfall the next day was relentless. People trekked through inches of the white stuff on sidewalks while their clothing gathered layers of it. Along the street, shopkeepers shoveled the path to their store entrance to keep pedestrians safe.

I left earlier to beat the traffic, but it soon became clear that everyone else on the road had the same idea. I arrived at the unit fifteen minutes late.

"Tough driving this morning, wasn't it?" Ryan looked up from his computer as I reached my desk.

"That's for sure."

"Don't feel bad. I got in five minutes ago myself." He smiled and went back to tapping on his keyboard.

I sat down and turned on my computer. It was my turn to cover incoming calls on the Info-Crime line this morning. Calls had trickled in since we launched Susan Kendall's page on the police website days ago, but the majority of callers had been curiosity seekers.

I answered today's first anonymous call ten minutes later.

"Hi," the man said. "I'm calling about Susan Kendall. I went to the same high school as her."

I sensed his sincerity and willingness to share information. "Can you tell me your name?" I asked, although he didn't have to reveal his identity.

"Well..." He hesitated. "I'll tell you my first name. It's Ernie."

Jennifer Sarto could probably help me find his full name from her photos or school records. "Ernie, how well did you know Susan?"

"I was a teenager and had a mad crush on her." A smile came through his words. "I was so happy when she accepted to go to the school prom with me on graduation night. Unfortunately, things got weird from the moment I picked her up."

My curiosity soared. "How?"

"She told me she'd meet me outside her house at a specific time that evening and not to ring the bell or knock. She had to wait until her father got drunk and fell asleep before she could sneak out. Believe me, it wasn't a fun night. We only spent three hours together."

"Did you see her again?"

"We dated a few times, but I broke it off by July."

"Why?"

Ernie sighed. "We were pretty close and all, but I felt that nothing positive could ever develop from our relationship. Not with a father like hers."

I understood what he was implying but asked anyway. "What do you mean?"

"The old man was very possessive of Susan's time. He'd go nuts if she didn't come home right after work to make dinner. He forced her to hand over her full pay every week. The guy was a scrooge. What's worse, I suspected that he..." He stopped.

"Go on."

"I'm sure her father beat her. She had these large bruises on her arms that..." He stopped again. "Anyway, if the old man is still alive, I hope he gets what's coming to him."

I didn't need an explanation. "What can you tell me about Lisa, her younger sister?"

"Nothing much," Ernie said. "I heard that she stayed with her father after Susan left home. The word in town was that he got into heavy drinking and couldn't hold a job. He sold the house, and the little girl went into foster care."

"Anything else you can tell me about Susan?"

"Nope. After I saw the police website about her, I felt it was my duty to call. I'm glad I got it off my chest. I hope you catch her killer." He ended the call.

Ryan glided his chair from behind his computer screen so he could see me. "That conversation sounded promising. Anything useful come out of it?"

I recounted the details. "The caller—Ernie—was honest. I'll ask Jennifer Sarto if she can find him in her school photos. The information we got from the people we interviewed so far, including this latest caller, proves one thing."

"What?"

"That the Kendall family's history of violence was common knowledge in Willowburg. It infuriates me how witnesses claim that Richard Kendall is a possible murderer, yet no one comes forward with solid proof." I clenched my hands in frustration.

"Either they don't have tangible evidence or they're afraid to come forward."

"It's mostly fear."

"These things take time, Amber," Ryan said, his voice calming. "Sooner or later, something will pop up to help us solve the case."

"You're right. I needed to blow off steam."

"We all get those days. Stay cool." He went back to work.

I called Jennifer Sarto to see if she could find the identity of the mysterious "Ernie" in her school records. She didn't answer the phone, so I left a message.

The next two hours brought nosy callers and nothing substantial. I was eager to hand over the line to Nadia for a morning break. I glanced at her desk. She wasn't there. While I waited for her to return, a call came in through the Info-Crime line. I took it.

"Your time is up," the caller said, his voice disguised with a modifying device. "You can stop playing those silly games."

"What?"

"You heard me." His voice was gruffer now. "Quit playing with matches. You'll burn yourself."

A perception of flames and smoke blinded me. "Stop it!" I shrieked, prompting Ryan to leap out of his chair.

"Don't bother tracing the call. It's a *burner* phone." The caller let out a hideous, mocking laugh before the line went dead.

Matches? Burn? These details were not a coincidence. No information regarding the burnt matches had ever been released to the public. The caller had to be connected to Susan Kendall's case and possibly the other two cold cases.

Ryan rushed to my side in two strides. "Are you okay?" Apprehension flashed in his brown eyes.

I took a shaky breath. "That last call... Listen to it."

He listened attentively to the recorded conversation, his brow furrowing with apprehension. "Sounds diabolical, but we could have a veritable lead here. Even a traceable one." He hurried over to Corey's desk and asked him to trace the call.

This last caller had to be someone close to our investigation. I had the distinct impression that either Ryan or I had interviewed him. In fact, I was positive we had.

Ryan hurried up to my desk. "Amber, did you get any perceptions from the caller's voice?"

"Like the other times, I sensed intense anger," I said. "Then I saw an image of fire and smoke. The caller has to be connected to the three cases we're investigating."

"Anything else?"

"Yes. He's one of the people we interviewed."

"You're not serious. Who?"

"I can't say for sure. I merely sensed that one of us has spoken with him before." I mentally scrolled through the list of our suspected individuals. "Can we eliminate Richard Kendall as a potential suspect? There was no phone in his room. He'd have to use the one at the front desk. I doubt he'd make a threatening call in the presence of other people."

"It doesn't mean he didn't have a burner phone hidden in his room," Ryan pointed out. "Unfortunately, we can't ask for a search warrant. We have no probable cause." He paused in thought. "The caller's mention of matches is interesting."

"And the way he laughed after he said it was a 'burner' phone. How horrid is that!" I shivered inwardly.

Corey came over to us and confirmed the call couldn't be traced. "The caller used a burner phone. He must have burned the phone number on his phone to erase all data."

"They usually do," Ryan said.

"Burned the phone number," I repeated. "What does that mean?"

Corey explained, "Let's say the caller instantly deletes his number in the phone settings after he hangs up. All his texts, calls, or voicemails then disappear. In other words, all history is gone." He said to Ryan, "There's another option. We can go the legal route and ask for a warrant to trace the connection through his app provider. It could take weeks or months, though."

"Okay," Ryan said. "Let's give it a try. Thanks, Corey."

Scenes from "The Little Match Girl" raced through my mind yet again: an abusive father...burnt matches...a young girl who dies in the snow, frozen to death. "Ryan, I need to defend my theory. I'm positive we're dealing with another serial killer who has a fondness for fairy tales."

He fixed a serious gaze on me. "It seems to be pointing in that direction, doesn't it? What we need are more leads to pin down the real perp. Maybe Matt dug up valuable info from his interviews. He should be back soon."

~

The sound of steps shuffling down the hallway reached us minutes later. Matt appeared around the corner, his face flushed. "I must have walked a mile in a foot of snow and battering winds. I had a hard time finding witness number six, the last of the witnesses. I thought I'd have to give up my search." He set an oversized coffee cup on his desk and his backpack on the floor. "In the end, I tracked her down to a new address." He sank into his chair.

Ryan asked, "What have you got?"

Matt wrapped his hands around his coffee cup. "Catherine Lambert was a sales attendant at a clothing store in Cedarberry. It's about an hour away from Trimville, the other town I visited. One evening after work, she took a shortcut home out the back of the store and through the alley. That's where she found our third victim, Pamela Cooper. Her hand was sticking out from under a pile of snow."

"What a horrible discovery!" I said, imagining the incident. "She must have been terrified."

"You bet," Matt said. "She told me she still has recurring nightmares about it. We have to find this guy."

"Our three murders have one significant element in common: three burnt matches were left with each victim," Ryan said. "The next step is to interpret the symbolism of these burnt matches."

"The killer was a heavy smoker?" Matt joked. "What do *you* think it means, Ryan? You're the expert when it comes to profiling these killers."

If I hadn't been familiar with Matt's frankness, I'd have interpreted his comment as an insult. But Matt being Matt, I took it as another shade of ignorance about Ryan's capabilities.

"It's a given that the perp didn't care about the victims," Ryan said, his tone even. "He wished they'd burn. There wasn't much chance of that happening in the snow, so he left the burnt matches behind as his signature, maybe to show he was in control of the situation."

"Yes, leaving the burnt matches next to the victim is symbolic," I said. "But since the stabbings show extreme rage, his connection to each of them might be more personal."

Ryan shook his head so-so. "If you're interpreting the murders are a revenge of sorts, I'm not so sure. I prefer the concept that the perp sized up his vulnerable victims and acted on that premise."

We were going in circles. To get another interpretation of the symbolism of the burnt matches, I needed to visit Laura King. She was a psychologist, historian, and my most trustworthy confidante. Unfortunately, I'd have to wait till Monday to contact her.

It was going to be a long weekend.

Right now, we had other problems to take care of. Ryan and I agreed that shoveling one car out of the parking lot was enough. I left mine there, surrounded by two feet of snow, while Ryan drove me home.

16

R yan reached for the bottle of red wine on the coffee table. "Want more wine, Amber?"

"Yes, please." I watched as he refilled my glass. The wine dulled my ability to capture psychic perceptions to a degree, but I welcomed the warm fuzzy feeling inside me. What better way to relax on a Friday evening after a hectic week.

He sat next to me on the sofa and stared at the wood fireplace we'd lit. My parents had opted for a wood-burning one rather than a gas fireplace decades ago. "Your fireplace crackles a lot."

"It's music to my ears."

He took a sip of wine and said nothing. Something was troubling him.

"You're unusually quiet this evening," I said.

Ryan drank more wine. "I have a few things on my mind."

"Like what?"

"Like the invitation to dinner tomorrow."

"From Uncle Ted? Why?"

"It doesn't sit well with me. With us."

Even though Ryan and I were secretly dating, we hadn't

planned on living together. Not yet anyway. We didn't want to take a chance to be found out and lose our jobs because of workplace rules that banned an intimate relationship between staff members.

I asked Ryan, "Are you worried my uncle will find out about us?"

His forehead creased with concern. "To begin with, I'm worried about the invitation. Why did he invite me?"

"It's a friendly gesture."

"Your uncle is the chief of police. He doesn't do 'friendly.' He's a tough dude."

Could he be right? If so, were our jobs at risk? We'd find out soon enough.

I'd completed my volunteer term visiting sick kids in hospitals and seniors in retirement homes, so I had more free time than usual on Saturday. Since my visits meant so much to the patients and gave me such pleasure in return, I vowed to seek out similar opportunities in the new year.

The exception was Mrs. Brody, Ryan's widowed mother, who suffered from dementia. We popped in to see her at the retirement home in the early afternoon. Her lapses in memory didn't deter her from recognizing Ryan and me, although she'd come up with a new name for me: Lily. We cut short our stay when she insisted on joining her friends at a bingo game.

Back at home, I sensed Ryan's uneasiness as the time neared for our dinner invitation. Although I shared the same fears, I held back from talking about it.

As we drove to our destination, Ryan said, "I think your uncle learned about our intimate relationship and is going to scold us like two kids who've done something wrong. Or maybe he's just going to flat out fire us."

"Let's not jump to conclusions," I said, trying to keep us both calm.

On our arrival, Uncle Ted and Aunt Elaine greeted me with hugs and shook hands with Ryan. The cordial welcome eased the tension somewhat, and I could feel my body relax.

During dinner, Aunt Elaine winked at me when no one else was looking. It was a sign that she was aware of my relationship with Ryan. She wanted my happiness above all, so I knew she'd protect my secret bond, even from Uncle Ted. But was her support enough to save our jobs?

The conversation centered on common topics throughout dinner, like fine wines, cars, and travel destinations. It was comforting to see a connection forming between Ryan and my family. Maybe this gathering wasn't about my relationship with Ryan after all. If so, we had nothing to fear.

After coffee and dessert were served, silence hung in the air. Uncle Ted cleared his throat, then said, "Rumors are circulating that have made their way to me. Disturbing rumors."

I gasped inwardly.

Aunt Elaine stared at Uncle Ted with a puzzled expression. "What rumors, Ted?"

"They're about Amber." His eyes were alert as he focused on me. "Someone is spreading gossip about your special gift and how our investigators depend on you for solving cold cases."

Oh, no! The rumors had reached the top of the echelon!

My throat tightened in disbelief, but I managed to say, "Uncle Ted, I'm so sorry."

"You're not to blame, Amber." Uncle Ted turned to Ryan. "Aside from the social benefit of this dinner, I invited you here tonight for another reason. The subject is a matter of privacy."

Uh-oh! Here it comes! Our jobs are lost!

"I was told that the personnel working at the unit were sworn to secrecy," Uncle Ted said. "Nevertheless, it's possible that someone leaked the word about Amber's psychic abilities."

His implication stunned me again. I was speechless.

Ryan jumped into action. "What can I do to help?"

"Start with the unit," Uncle Ted said. "See what you can find out from the staff there. If we determine that the source is from outside the unit, it demands a different strategy. At that point, we'll need to broaden our investigation to the entire division."

"There are trustworthy people I can rely on," Ryan said with confidence.

"Good. Above all, it's imperative that Amber remains safe."

I found my voice and addressed the two men at the table. "Don't I have a say in this? Please don't talk about me as if I'm not here."

Aunt Elaine placed a gentle hand on my arm. "Your uncle is concerned for your welfare, dear. Who knows what can happen if the wrong person finds out about your gift."

She was right. Safety first. I had to be more rational about it, like Uncle Ted and Ryan.

"There's something else we can do to protect you, Amber." Uncle Ted grew pensive. "I suggest hiring a bodyguard, perhaps someone from a private agency to escort you."

His idea of protecting me had gone too far. "It's not necessary," I protested. "I'm very careful. I make sure I'm not being followed."

Ryan disagreed with Uncle Ted for his own reasons. "Being escorted around by someone unfamiliar will bring more attention to Amber."

Uncle Ted eyed him with interest. "Do you have another suggestion?"

"I'll do it instead. I'll take on the task to protect Amber. I'll drive her to work and back home."

"I don't want to interfere with your personal life."

His personal life? Was that a hint that Uncle Ted was aware of our relationship?

If Ryan had interpreted my uncle's comment in the same way I had, he didn't show it. In a composed manner, he said,

"It's not a problem. We work in the same unit and on the same cases. We can easily arrange a mutual work schedule."

"Consider it done. Thank you, Ryan." Uncle Ted gave him a nod, then reached for the bottle of sherry and served it in crystal glasses.

This new "bodyguard" arrangement with Ryan would camouflage my relationship with him, no questions asked from anyone. If Uncle Ted was the least bit aware of my secret connection with Ryan, he'd hidden it well.

On the drive home, my thoughts buzzed with the possibility that someone at the unit had leaked details about more than my psychic abilities. I said to Ryan, "The anonymous call to the Info-Crime line the other day wasn't a coincidence. The caller's talk about matches and burning... I'd hate to find out that he got inside information about Susan's case from someone at the unit."

"I want to trust the staff," Ryan said, "but I need to find the source of the leak about you. It means putting trust aside and questioning each one of them."

I feared the consequences of interviewing our coworkers. It would be a blatant show of mistrust in them and could complicate our interactions with them. On the other hand, if we discovered that the leak didn't come from the staff in our immediate circle, Ryan faced an uphill battle in locating the outside source.

17

I was eager to spend Sunday afternoon with Nicole Latour, my best friend. I welcomed the chance to catch up on recent events in our lives. Although Nicole lived a short walk from my house, Ryan insisted on dropping me off. "Your safety is my priority," he said, reminding me of his new role as my bodyguard.

It was a stress-release kind of day and my turn to visit Nicole at her place. She'd provide the snacks for our get-together, but it didn't stop me from arriving at her door with a jar of her favorite chewy gumdrops.

I loved the way she'd decorated her apartment with contemporary furniture in earthy tones. The overall style was a contrast to the traditional furniture I'd inherited from my parents. What made it more interesting each time I visited her was that she'd added something new, no matter how tiny it was.

I pointed out the miniature Japanese vase in reds, yellows, and blues on a side table in the living room. "Is that another gift from your secret admirer?"

"Oh, Amber, there is no secret admirer," Nicole said in her charming French-Canadian accent.

"You bought it?"

"No." She sighed. "Okay, if you must know, the vase was a gift from the father of one of my students. He was late and asked me to watch over his little boy for an extra hour or so. No big deal." Holding the jar of gumdrops, she sat down next to me on the sofa.

"Is the boy's father a single parent?"

Her face reflected surprise. "Yes. How did you know?"

I shrugged. "Just a guess."

She waved a forefinger at me. "Now, Amber, don't start getting any ideas. A handsome man like him? He must have a girlfriend. Or two." She giggled, then swiftly changed the subject as she opened the jar of gumdrops. "How is it going with you and Ryan?"

"It's good."

"Good? That's all? I was expecting to see an engagement ring on your finger by now, no?" Nicole's accent coupled with her natural curiosity endeared her to me even more.

I laughed. "Hold on. I told you how Ryan and I had agreed to take it slowly."

"Okay, but don't go so slow that you come to a full stop."

I laughed again. "We won't."

She held out the jar of gumdrops. When I declined, she popped one into her mouth. "So? What else is new? How is your job going?"

Nicole didn't know the exact nature of my job at the unit and how involved I was in solving cold cases. She knew nothing about my psychic abilities either. It was for her own safety that I withheld these pieces of information from her. I told her I worked in an administrative position and witnessed the gory details of criminal cases on paper only.

"My job? The usual stuff." I played it casual, hoping she'd drop the subject. She didn't.

"I told you this before," she said between chews. "If I had your job, it would affect me so much. Ugh!" She shuddered for dramatic effect. "I would have nightmares. How do you manage to sleep at night?"

"You get used to the...um...details in investigative files after you read about them so often."

"Oh, that reminds me," Nicole said. "I looked up the Montreal police website this week. Not that I like to visit that site, but at least I can see what kind of files you're working on."

"What page did you visit?"

"It was a new page for that girl in a town who was murdered around Christmas in the 1980s. Susan... I can't remember her last name."

"Susan Kendall."

"That's it," Nicole said. "Poor girl. What kind of a person does such a horrible thing?"

"It's a cruel way to die," I said.

"Especially around the Christmas holidays." She tsk-tsked before chewing another gumdrop. "I hope people will call the Info-Crime number to help the police solve this murder."

Although I was counting on evidence and tips from callers to lead us to Susan's killer, I welcomed a different perspective from a person I trusted. I was counting on psychologist Laura King to steer me in the right direction.

18

Ryan stopped in front of the medical building at eight o'clock Monday morning. It was our first day back at work under the new arrangement that Uncle Ted had authorized. In addition to bodyguard, my investigative partner and secret lover had now taken on the role of my chauffeur. In reality, I had no choice. I'd abandoned my snowbound car in the police parking lot Friday evening.

"I'll pick you up in an hour," Ryan said before I stepped out of the car. "Call me if your appointment takes longer."

I'd told Ryan I had a doctor's appointment. It was a little white lie. Then again, it wasn't a lie at all. Laura King, a psychologist and old family friend, was indeed a doctor. Other titles she carried included historian and fairy-tale expert. The latter was the real reason I sought her advice on specific cold cases and why I requested to see her today.

I sat in one of two comfy armchairs across from Laura's desk. Because of the trust between us, I shared the details of Susan Kendall's case with her but left out the names. "The elements remind me of the fairy tale, 'The Little Match Girl.'

Since I don't want to jump to conclusions, I'd welcome your opinion."

Laura steepled her fingers. "Although the elements in your case don't completely mirror the fairy tale you mentioned, there are striking similarities. The character in 'The Little Match Girl' was poor and hungry as she tried to sell the matches. The victim in your cold case went hungry at times as she struggled to make a life for herself."

"There was family abuse," I said.

"Yes. The character in 'The Little Match Girl' was indeed a victim of abuse, which is not unique. A dysfunctional family can be found in numerous fairy tales. For example, Cinderella is abused by her stepmother and two stepsisters. However, as in those fairy tales, the victim in your cold case found a way out and had hope of redemption."

"How?"

"Your victim escaped from her father's cruelty when she moved out of the house at eighteen years old. As in 'The Little Match Girl' where her loving grandmother brings the girl to a hopeful place away from poverty and misery, your victim met a wealthy boyfriend who offered her hope for a better life."

"But my victim was murdered. Where's the hope?"

"Granted, it exists in fairy tales that have happily-ever-after endings," Laura said. "They represent the spiritual triumph of good over evil. They offer a way out and the expectation of redemption. However, the genre is becoming darker, like some world events. That's where perpetrators come in today with their own interpretations of fairy tales, their own twisted ideas of how they can ensure that redemption."

I had more questions for Laura. "What about the burnt matches? Is there any symbolism to them?"

"The matches in 'The Little Match Girl' symbolize hope and comfort. Even while they're being destroyed, they give off warmth and light. In your cold case, the perpetrator burns all hope by extinguishing the matches. It's his way of showing control over the victim."

Ryan had mentioned a similar interpretation. I shared an additional theory with Laura. "Could the murder be personal?"

"Yes. The burnt matches can represent the anger and revenge the killer felt toward his victim. *Burn in hell* is his message. That he wasn't afraid to leave the matches at the crime scene is an indication of his confidence. Perhaps he even made sure he left no fingerprints on them."

Forensics hadn't delivered a report on the burnt matches, so I couldn't confirm fingerprints or traces of DNA one way or the other. "What does the killer gain by leaving the matches with his victim?"

Laura sat back in her chair. "To the killer, the matches symbolize a lasting achievement. It's possible that he sees himself as a liberator for his victims."

"A liberator? That's a frightening thought."

"Their minds don't work the same way ours do. He interprets it this way: Even though the matches burn out, the flame of his achievements will stay in his memory forever."

"From what you're saying, we could be looking at another killer with a fairy-tale leaning."

"It's a strong possibility." Laura checked her watch, a sign that she was running out of time for my free session.

I chose my next question carefully. "Do serial killers ever stop killing?"

"Yes, they're known to stop for periods of time, sometimes years, before they resume killing. Perhaps they get married and have a family or find other ways to express control. They usually stop when they get too old to dispose of their victims themselves."

"What other traits should I expect to find in this killer?"

"You might recall from our previous discussions that the perpetrator can be a helpful neighbor, a friendly store clerk, or someone with a decent reputation. An overall respectable guy.

Remember, appearances can be deceiving." She stopped. "Listen to me giving you advice that you don't need. Amber, I'm confident that your experience and special insights will guide you in that respect, like they have in the past." She smiled.

"Thanks, Laura." I returned a smile.

"By the way, have your nightmares diminished since we last spoke about them?"

"Somewhat," I lied, not wanting to get into that topic. "Working on cold cases helps me to confront my ghosts."

"I'm pleased to hear that."

"How is your secret thesis going? The interpretation of fairy tales in modern society."

"Oh, that." Laura dismissed the subject with a shake of her head. "My research has introduced me to a maze of information over the years. The manuscript is nowhere near ready for publication."

"I'm sure it'll be a success." I stood up. "Thanks for your time."

She walked around her desk and gave me a hug. "Don't be a stranger. I'm here if you need me."

19

———

I couldn't wait to share my theory with Ryan. My meeting with Laura King had solidified my suspicions that we were dealing with a serial killer who used fairy tales as a basis for murdering young women.

Ryan picked me up in front of the medical building. "Did everything go okay?"

I'd almost forgotten I'd told him my appointment was for an annual physical exam. "Yes," I said. "Everything's okay."

He kept his eyes on me, as if he were waiting for me to say more, but I didn't elaborate. I pulled out my phone and casually scanned my email messages.

Moments after we'd driven off, I launched my concept. "Ryan, I have a theory about the matches that the killer left near the bodies of our three victims."

"Is this a delayed reaction from one of your insights?" he asked.

"You could say that." It was Laura's theory, but I held back from sharing my source with him. I didn't want to betray her trust in me. "Similar to the other fairy-tale cases we've solved, the potential suspect in Susan Kendall's case sees himself as the savior of his victims. The burnt matches are a sign that he achieved his goal."

"Go on."

"He extinguishes the matches and leaves them near his victims. It can be a sign he's extinguishing all hope and showing his control over them."

Ryan weighed my theory. "You're sounding more convinced than ever that we have another fairy-tale killer on our hands."

"Definitely," I said with more confidence than ever.

"In that case, I'll have to give it more consideration."

He remained silent during the rest of the drive to work. Aside from mulling over my theory, he had other things on his mind. His investigation into the mysterious leak about my psychic gift that had reached my uncle, the chief of police, was at the top of his list.

As soon as we arrived at the office, Ryan and I arranged a meeting with Nadia and Corey. We needed to find out if they had, by accident or not, mentioned my psychic abilities to anyone outside the unit. Ryan wanted me to attend so that I could pick up on whether they were lying or not. As serious as the breach was, I was worried they might lose their jobs over a possible slip-up. I didn't want to be responsible for that.

First up was Nadia. She took a seat at the conference table across from Ryan and me. "Is there a new development?" she asked, as if she were expecting an update on a case.

"No." Ryan went straight to the point. "We have reason to suspect a probable leak in the unit."

Nadia's brown eyes went wide. "A leak? About what?"

"About Amber's special talent."

"Who's behind the leak?"

"We thought you would be able to tell us."

Nadia blinked as she processed the accusation behind his words. "You think it's me?" She placed a hand on her throat in a protective gesture. "Ryan, I'd never do such a thing." She looked at me. "Amber, I swore not to tell anyone about your...um...abilities. I promise you I haven't."

"Any idea who might have?"

"No, not at all." She stared at us. "Is there anything I can do to help?"

"Not at the moment." Ryan dismissed her and opened the door. He'd asked Corey to wait outside the conference room to prevent any exchange of conversation between him and Nadia on her way out.

The young information officer slid his lanky frame into the chair that Nadia had vacated moments earlier. "You wanted to talk to me?"

"We suspect there's been a leak of information from someone in the unit," Ryan said to him.

Cory stiffened. "What kind of leak?"

"A leak about Amber's psychic abilities. She's been put at risk."

"It wasn't me," Corey said, adjusting his eyeglasses. "No way. I wouldn't betray Amber."

Ryan asked him the same question that he asked Nadia. "Any idea who might have leaked the information?"

"No. Is there anything I can do to help find the source?"

"Keep it under wraps for now. That's all."

After Corey left and closed the door behind him, Ryan asked me, "What do your instincts tell you?"

"They're both telling the truth," I said.

"I agree."

"If the leak didn't come from Nadia or Corey, where did it come from?"

"There might be one other source." Ryan pursed his lips. "Matt."

"He does seem a little cynical about my capabilities," I said, "but we shouldn't assume he'd betray me."

"I'll ask him anyway." He reached over and squeezed my

hand. "I don't want you to worry about this anymore. I promise you I'll find the leak."

His assurance didn't quell my fears. I needed a change of topic. "Let's go back to our desks. Matt should be here by now. I'll share my theory about Susan's killer with him."

Matt was sitting at his desk, a doughnut and a large cup of coffee before him. As we approached, he said, "Hey, guys. I was wondering what you've been up to."

"There's something we'd like to run by you," I said, swiveling my chair to face his.

Ryan rolled his chair over to join us and sat down. "Amber came up with a theory about Susan Kendall's killer."

"It's about the matches he left behind with his victims." I explained the theory about the killer seeing himself as their savior and leaving burnt matches at the crime scene to show he attained his goal.

Matt listened intently, then said, "That's wild! From my experience in homicide, killers try their best *not* to leave evidence at the scene of the crime."

"That's the usual scenario," Ryan said. "The difference with some of these perps is that they perceive themselves as saviors, like Amber pointed out. Consequently, they take pride in leaving their signature as a claim to their victims. Our perp might have kept the rest of the matchbook as a souvenir."

"Why?"

"To relive the moment of excitement from the killing. In essence, to relive his fantasies."

I winced. "How gruesome! And risky."

"They're bold enough to trust they can get away with it," Ryan said. "They enjoy taunting the police in the process. My belief is we're dealing with the same perp for all three victims."

"One who's a chain-smoker," Matt said.

"Not necessarily," Ryan said. "He could have left the matches as a symbolic gesture. Even so, we'll keep the possibility he's a smoker on our radar."

"Anything else?" Matt asked.

Ryan leaned toward him and kept his voice low. "On another topic... We believe there's a leak of information in the unit." He brought him up to date.

"It wasn't me." Matt raised a thumb in the direction of Corey and Nadia and whispered, "Did you ask them?"

"Yes, they denied it."

"Amber, maybe you happened to mention it to someone without thinking," Matt said.

"I wouldn't do that," I retorted.

"Matt, everyone in the unit is in the clear," Ryan said. "We need to find the external source, plain and simple. I'll reach out to my contacts outside the unit to see what I can find out."

Everyone in the unit had witnessed firsthand how I captured insights from pieces of physical evidence and my emotional response to what I experienced. How an outside source had acquired this inside knowledge was a puzzle. How far it could have extended was even more disturbing.

The way I saw it, Ryan's options were limited when it came to finding the leak. Would anyone admit they were guilty? Not a chance. Trying to contain a message that had potentially spread like wildfire by now was the problem.

I had ample reason to worry.

20

———

After Ryan returned from a meeting with homicide detectives the next morning, he met with Matt and me in the conference room behind closed doors. With a grim expression, he took a seat facing us and placed a folder on the table. His silence told me he was having a hard time coming forward with what he wanted to discuss.

It was unlike Ryan not to make eye contact or offer an initial bit of conversation before we sat down to a meeting. His unusual behavior put me on edge. I wasn't alone.

"What's the matter?" Matt's tone was apprehensive. "You look like you lost your best friend."

"I'll be direct." Lines gathered along Ryan's brow. "I met with a couple of investigators in homicide earlier. They asked if we're using psychics to help solve our cases."

My pulse sped up. "No!"

"You've got to be kidding," Matt said.

"I'm not." Ryan stared at Matt. "I made it clear that no one outside the unit should know about Amber."

Matt held up both hands. "I already told you it wasn't me. I swear."

Whether or not he believed Matt, Ryan said nothing and appeared to drop the subject.

I, on the other hand, was still reeling from the news. "What did you say to your contacts, Ryan?"

"I covered up," he said. "I told them they were dreaming...that they shouldn't listen to rumors. I think I convinced them."

I had my doubts. "What if your tactic doesn't work? What if they trust their source more than they trust you?"

Ryan squared his shoulders, his posture confident. "I'll do whatever I have to do, Amber."

Anxiety rose inside me. "What does that mean?"

"I'll find another way to protect you from the gossip."

"Ryan, you're just like my ex-wife." Matt crossed his arms, sulking.

"What are you talking about?"

"She blamed me for everything that went wrong. You blamed me for the leak moments ago. You owe me an apology."

"You're right, Matt. My apologies." Ryan stood up. "Can you excuse us? I need to discuss another case with Amber."

After Matt left, Ryan picked up the folder he'd brought into the room earlier. He circled the table and sat in a chair next to me.

I wasn't ready to discuss a new case. I hadn't moved past the topic of the leak yet. "Before we discuss this other case—"

"It's okay. There's no other case. I wanted to talk to you about something else."

"I need to say one more thing first."

"Go ahead."

"We've eliminated everyone in the unit who might have leaked the word about me and my abilities. What if someone accidentally mentioned it without realizing it?"

Ryan's gaze dropped to the floor. "I've been trying to figure it out. I was hoping the leak had come from someone else. Then I realized it was me."

I froze. "You? Why would you say that? You've been protecting my secret from the start."

He gave me a shy smile. "I admit I raved about your talent for solving crimes to a former colleague in homicide."

"That's okay. It's not the same as saying I was psychic and captured scary images from criminal evidence."

"No, but he told me he found it strange that you were hired as a consultant, seeing as you had no previous experience as a police investigator."

"How did he know that?"

"I told him," Ryan said, bowing his head. "I backed it up by saying you had an inborn talent. A gut feeling about things. I guess he took it and ran with it."

"Oh." I felt as if the bottom had dropped out of my safety net.

He went on. "I confronted him afterward and was able to contain it. He could have spoken to others in the meantime, though. I'm so sorry, Amber."

"The question is, how far has it spread? Do we have an idea?"

"No." He took my hands in his. "Don't worry. No matter what, I'm here for you."

I'd managed to keep my secret within the confines of work-related structures. Now it had spread beyond those limits. First, there was Uncle Ted's revelation about the leak. Then there was Ryan's validation that the gossip about my psychic abilities could have circulated far and fast.

I trusted Ryan, but with rumors spreading about me, in addition to the recent phone threats, was his protection enough to save my job? To save me?

Damn! As if I didn't have enough to worry about.

21

I looked forward to the interview that Nadia had scheduled for us this afternoon. Anything to take my mind off the leak about my "inborn talent"—as Ryan put it—scattering in all directions like millions of flurries in a snowstorm.

As Ryan steered the car along the streets of east-end Montreal, my thoughts swung to our impending visit with Susan Kendall's sister. Lisa's extended work shifts at the hospital had prevented Nadia from scheduling an interview with her sooner. Seeing as I'd established a rapport with Lisa through the Info-Crime line, Ryan suggested that I initiate the questions rather than him.

Now fifty-seven years old, Lisa had weathered the years gracefully. Soft highlights in her shoulder-length hair complemented a fair skin and blue eyes. Having been removed from her father's house and placed under foster care when she was a young teen had most likely spared her years of anxiety.

She led us into a tidy kitchen where we settled around a wood table that seated four. A stack of letters, bound by a red ribbon, was the sole item on the table.

Lisa put a hand on the pile. "After I agreed to meet with you,

I took out the letters Susan had sent me when we were both teenagers. There could be something in them that's useful for your investigation. I also included photos of Susan taken in her last months." She pulled out two photos from the pile. Susan's endearing smile, rosy cheeks, and long blonde hair spelled approachable. It was obvious that men would be attracted to her. Lisa tucked the photos back into the stack and slid it across the table to me.

"Thank you." I refrained from touching the letters. They could trigger emotions beyond my control. Instead, I said to Lisa, "Tell me about Kenneth Cameron, the man Susan dated."

Lisa smiled. "It seems like yesterday when Susan called to tell me she was leaving town with Kenneth. She sounded so happy and excited about her new life with him."

"Did Susan date other men before she met Kenneth?"

"You bring back memories," she said, pushing a strand of hair behind one ear. "There were a few young men, but none of them had staying power like Kenneth. Not that they wanted to stick around." She rolled her eyes.

"What do you mean?"

"Susan had to sneak out to meet them. She had to wait until Dad fell asleep drunk. When she had the time, she'd share stories about her outings with me."

I gestured toward the stack of letters. "When did Susan send you these letters?"

"After she left home that summer," Lisa said. "She was eighteen and I was fifteen. It was a tearful separation. She didn't want to see Dad anymore. Calling me at the house was risky in case he'd pick up the phone and listen. She sent me letters instead. I'd get to the mailbox before Dad, so he never found out about them. Her letters kept coming even after I was living in foster care. She was afraid that we'd lose our connection to each other." She sighed. "I'm glad Dad didn't see them. It was all for the better."

"In what way?"

"Susan wrote about how sorry she was that we couldn't see each other because of Dad. She had money problems but didn't want him to find out. She was working hard at the local diner to make ends meet, and a woman there helped her with lodging. I can't remember her name, but Susan mentioned her in the letters."

It had to be Debra. I guided the conversation back to a much closer friend of Susan's. "When did Kenneth come into the picture?"

"Later that summer. What an impression he made on Susan!" Lisa giggled. "She kept writing about how wonderful he was, how he left her generous tips, how he invited her on dates..." The joy on her face faded. "The last time I heard from Susan was when she phoned home. She told me she was quitting her job and leaving town with Kenneth that same night. They were planning to get married." Her eyes teared up.

I waited, sensing the pain that our conversation instilled in her. Hers was a multiple anguish: the loss of a close sister at a young age, a mother who died too soon, and a father she detested who had given her up to strangers.

She took out a tissue and dabbed at her eyes, then crumpled the tissue in her hand. "Susan shared something else with me that night." She sniffed. "She told me she was pregnant."

Her disclosure that Susan had shared the news about her pregnancy with her astounded me. Ryan stirred beside me, equally surprised.

"I was so happy for Susan," Lisa said. "I wished her good luck. She promised she'd call me later that week." She swallowed hard. "What happened afterward was terrifying. Dad had come home earlier than usual and had listened to our conversation on the extension phone downstairs. I hadn't heard him come in or the click on the phone when he picked up the receiver."

So that's how Richard found out about his daughter's pregnancy!

"After Susan hung up," Lisa said, "Dad was so angry. He ranted about how she had destroyed the family reputation, how he couldn't stand with pride beside his churchgoing neighbors anymore, and so on."

"Did he...hurt you?" I asked.

"No, Dad never laid a finger on me. I made sure to get out of his way when he was in a bad mood. After his temper tantrum that day, I stayed in my bedroom until it was time for me to prepare dinner. After dinner, he drank himself into oblivion and fell asleep in the living room, like he did every night."

Ryan joined the conversation. "He didn't leave the house that evening?"

"I don't think so," Lisa said, sounding uncertain. "The winds were so strong, I wouldn't have heard him leave anyway." She stared into the distance, as if she were remembering something else. "Kenneth. He knocked at the door that night. I was in my bedroom upstairs. Dad opened the door and shouted obscenities at the poor guy. He threatened him and chased him into the snowstorm. I ran to the window and saw Kenneth drive away."

"Was Susan with him?"

"I couldn't tell. It was dark and snowing hard. I was hoping she was in the car, but then I figured Kenneth wouldn't have driven all the way to the house asking about her." Her eyes reddened as she fought back the tears. "Unless they had come over to say goodbye."

Ryan leaned forward. "What time did Kenneth come to your house?"

"Late. Around ten o'clock, I think."

I was curious. "Did you ever see Kenneth again?" I asked Lisa.

"Yes," she said. "It was at the funeral services we held for Susan. He was crying. He told me he was so sorry about what happened. He said he had delayed his medical studies and joined the family business instead." She blinked hard, the tears streaming down her cheeks. "Things could have worked out so differently if he'd been on time to meet my sister that Christmas Eve. They would have left town, got married, had children and grandchildren like I did." She gestured toward the photos of two adults and two young children on magnets decorating the fridge door.

I could barely contain the angst welling up inside me. I clutched the amethyst crystal in my pocket to soothe my grief. Lisa's grief.

Ryan gave me a temporary reprieve. "Lisa, we understand that your father sold the home soon after and handed you over to government foster care."

"That's right," she said. "He couldn't afford the bills and hardly worked because of his drinking habit. In a way, he did me a favor. My foster parents gave me a good life. Years later, because of my horrid experience at home with Dad, I took a job in an orphanage. I wanted to give back to the community, as they say. Ironically, that's where I saw Kenneth one last time."

My curiosity surged. "Did Kenneth speak with you then?"

"No," Lisa said. "He didn't recognize me. He was with his wife. The couple left with three young siblings they had adopted. A two-year-old boy and two girls, three and four years old. The children's parents had died in a car crash." She grew pensive. "I guess Kenneth's wife wasn't able to have children of her own."

The truth could only be told by the people who knew it, but I wasn't about to share it with Lisa. "Is there anything else you'd like to tell us?"

Lisa grew teary again. "I feel guilty, as if I let Susan down after she took care of me all those years. I was the lucky one who didn't get hurt. In a physical sense, at least. You know what I mean?"

"Yes," I said. *Emotional scars.* I'd carried a similar guilt for years since the day my parents were murdered. I was spared their fate because I'd hidden in a secret compartment that my father had built in my bedroom closet. Frequent nightmares still reminded me of that horrid event.

I revisited a subject that Lisa had mentioned during her previous phone call to the Info-Crime line. "Your mother's accident when she fell down the stairs... Did you witness it?"

"No, I was in my bedroom," she said. "I heard her scream and then a heavy thump. By the time I went down, she was at the bottom of the stairs and not moving."

"Was anyone else with you?"

"No. Susan had classes. She was in high school. Dad was working in the backyard."

"Why weren't you in school?"

"I was sick that day."

Ryan had one last question for Lisa. "Do you have any idea who might have killed Susan?"

She raised her hands, palms out. "Be forewarned, I'm not accusing him, but my father had a terrible temper. I had to tiptoe around certain issues so as not to annoy him. My mother and Susan were more outspoken and paid the price."

"Do you think your father was angry enough to kill Susan?"

She gave Ryan a pointed look. "That's up to you to find out, isn't it?"

Ryan and I spent the last hour of our working day in the conference room reading Susan's letters to Lisa. Her words revealed loyalty and love for her younger sister, the promise they'll see each other soon, and the optimism of a new life with Kenneth.

A mix of deep sadness, anger, and exasperation swept over me. Alone with Ryan, I let the tears flow to release my pent-up emotions. A ruthless killer had destroyed a young woman's dreams in a brief moment of terror. The vicious ending to

Susan's life convinced me all the more that I needed to find him and bring him to justice.

22

Nadia contacted the unit the next morning to say she wasn't coming to work until after noon. Corey had taken the call and mumbled something about Nadia having to go to a doctor's appointment.

She'd rarely missed a day of work, so I was surprised until my radar kicked in. It wasn't a doctor's appointment. Something else had forced Nadia to take time off.

To define it as a busy morning was an understatement. Matt was helping Corey to input information on the police website for his two cold case victims. With Nadia away, Corey also had to upload photos of Susan Kendall and history information to the police website. Ryan was updating Susan's investigative file on his computer. With no other choice, I offered to replace Nadia and handle incoming calls on the Info-Crime line until she arrived.

I welcomed switching gears for a while. Answering anonymous phone calls provided variety and the occasional tip, though the latter failed to produce anything tangible lately. Like the frigid weather, our investigations were frozen in a holding pattern with no new leads in sight. I hadn't heard back from former schoolteacher Jennifer Sarto either, so I left another message on her voicemail.

It was almost noon when an incoming call arrived. I answered.

"I'm calling to say I knew the Kendall family years ago." The older woman's voice was hoarse. "I worked for a charity and heard about their unfortunate financial situation through the organization. They were on the list for food donations. Anyway, what I'm calling about is Susan Kendall's case."

"Do you have information that would help us?" I asked her.

"He was a cruel man."

"Who?"

"Her father."

"Richard Kendall?"

My mention of his name aroused Ryan's curiosity. He stole a look at me from behind his computer screen.

"I don't understand why his wife stayed with him all those years," the woman said. "Maybe because of the children." She coughed. "Truth be told, I didn't like the man. If he happened to be there when I'd drop off food supplies, I didn't dillydally. I left right away."

Even though the caller was heading in a different direction with her story, I let her continue. There had to be more.

"I went there with a food basket one afternoon," she said. "Mrs. Kendall told me her family wasn't a charity case and to stop dropping off food at their home. She was quite rude about it, not like her usual self. She didn't fool me one bit. I knew very well where that remark came from. Her husband, that's who. The word in town was that he beat his wife and Susan. I can vouch for that. Every time I visited Mrs. Kendall, she had a new bruise on her arm. Anyway, I never went back there after she practically threw me out. Why take a chance on her husband attacking me?"

I guided the conversation back to the cold case victim. "Do you know anyone who would want to harm Susan Kendall?"

"Weren't you listening to what I said about Richard Kendall, her own father?" Before I could answer, she blurted, "Here's another thing. I don't believe his wife fell down a flight of stairs. Lord, forgive me, but I wouldn't put it past her husband to have pushed her." She coughed. "And maybe, just maybe, he did Susan in too. I hope he rots in hell!"

The line went dead.

Ryan hurried over and peered down at me. "Another threatening call?"

"Not exactly." I summarized the conversation for him. "My sense is that the caller was sincere. What baffles me is the increasing number of witnesses who claim Richard Kendall could have killed his own daughter. What do you make of it?"

"We can't let it influence our investigation," he said. "However, we can assume that those who knew the Kendall family will voice their opinions based on personal experience. In some cases, gossip. We can't do anything until we have solid evidence against him."

"I'm with you on that, but all these people who come forward now... Where were they back then?"

"You know the answer. Past investigators ran out of time and money. That's why there are hundreds of cold cases in the storage room. It's up to us to investigate them, one by one. It'll take time."

Ryan was right, of course. More time and patience were what we needed. And a worthwhile lead.

"Sorry, Ryan," I said. "Sometimes I can't help feeling frustrated."

"We can only do the best we can." He returned to his desk.

Prank callers and curiosity-seekers filled the next hours. Two more anonymous callers commented about having known the victim but didn't provide any leads or were afraid to. Critical questions surfaced as well:

"Why is it taking so long for the police to solve this case?"

"The killer had to be someone Susan knew. Don't investigators have a list of suspects?"

"Are police investigators working full-time on this case?"

My answer to each question was the same: "We're doing our best. Thank you for calling the Info-Crime line."

Did I believe we were doing our best? If perseverance, sleepless nights, and a quest for justice had anything to do with it, then yes. As trite as it might sound, the only other solution would be an unforeseen stroke of good luck.

23

———

Nadia arrived at the unit shortly after noon. She exchanged several words with Corey before she sat down at her desk and started to work. Her bloodshot eyes projected sadness, as though she'd recently cried or was on the verge of crying. Her long hair was tied back, she hadn't applied makeup or eyeliner, and her complexion was paler than usual.

I regretted having to dump more work on her desk. She and Corey were already under pressure to upload information from hundreds of case files in the storage room to our database. Ryan, Matt, and I were under a related pressure. Since a considerable portion of the handwritten notes in the old files were illegible or incomplete, we needed to clarify the information before handing the files over to the duo for input.

As I held out a stack of files to Nadia, my hand brushed against hers. I perceived an image of her standing in front of a coffin. I couldn't see the deceased but got the impression he was a young man with whom she'd had a close relationship. It explained her grief. It was none of my business, so I let it go at that.

Matt took the rest of the afternoon off to bring his kids to dentist appointments. His ex-wife had performed this parental task the last time, so it was his turn. Ryan was busy completing reports for the lieutenant. Corey and Nadia were uploading case files to the database and agreed to work overtime to meet the lieutenant's quota.

Since everyone else was on a mission of sorts, I handled sporadic calls on the Info-Crime line and reviewed details in the case files. The off-site operator for the early evening shift would soon take over incoming calls. With fifteen minutes to go, I answered what I expected would be my last call.

"You don't listen very well, do you?" The raspy male voice grated my ears.

"Excuse me?"

"You heard me. It's time to stop playing games. Your investigation will get you nowhere." His voice grew gruffer. "Stop investigating Susan's case or you'll regret it. That goes for every one of you over there—but especially you!"

An image of a man holding a large knife flashed through my mind. He was coming straight at me!

"No!" I gasped for air.

"I missed my first target, but I won't the next time!" A click sounded at the other end of the line. He was gone.

Ryan rushed over to me. "It was him again, wasn't it?"

I nodded and tried to breathe normally. "He...he threatened us."

As Ryan listened to the recording, shock spread over his face. "Damn! He threatened the entire unit. I have to put everyone on high alert." He sent out an urgent text message to staff in the division about the potential threat. Although he knew it was useless, he asked Corey to trace the call anyway.

"What did the caller mean by missing his first target?" I asked Ryan. "No one here has been hurt."

Lines formed across his forehead. "Whatever he's talking about, we'd better watch our backs."

Corey walked up to us moments later. "Sorry, Ryan. No luck

in tracing that anonymous call. I went the legal route like we did for the last anonymous caller."

"Okay. Thanks."

"By the way, I got the urgent message you sent out," Corey said. "What's the plan?"

"We'll need to—"

Nadia dashed over to us. "Ryan, I received your message. What's going on?"

Ryan repeated bits of conversation from the latest threatening call to the Info-Crime line. Startled gapes from Nadia and Corey heightened my fears.

What no one expected next was Nadia bursting into tears. "My boyfriend," she said. "He died last night. He was struck by a hit-and-run driver." She pulled out a tissue and dabbed at the tears.

Nadia's boyfriend! He was the deceased young man in the impression I'd captured earlier.

I felt her profound grief. "Nadia, I'm so sorry for your loss." I touched her arm.

"Thank you."

"My sympathies, Nadia," Ryan added. "Can you tell us what happened?"

Between sobs, she said, "We were leaving the restaurant and walking along the sidewalk. It was late at night. Andrew pushed me out of the way of a car that was coming right at us. The driver hit him and sped off. The ambulance arrived quickly, but it was too late." She trembled and fought to compose herself. "Andrew saved my life. After what you told me, Ryan, that hit was meant for me!"

My heart hammered in my chest as I sensed her anxiety. She was right. The threats were happening!

"Did you file a police report?" Ryan asked Nadia.

"Yes," she said, tears streaking her makeup. "I couldn't even describe the car. It was snowing, and everything happened so fast."

"Do you know the police officer's name?"

"It's Chris Farand."

"Okay. I'll follow through with him and ask for a copy of the report."

"Thank you."

Ryan frowned. "It might be a good idea if you went home now, Nadia. Take a couple of days off, if you need to."

"I don't want to slack off on my work," she said, raising her chin. "I'll be back here tomorrow morning."

"Okay. I'll request a police escort for you right now and tomorrow morning. For you, too, Corey."

"Thanks," Corey said, swallowing hard. "I'd feel a heck of a lot safer."

Ryan arranged for police cruisers to escort them home immediately. He promised to bring everyone up to date with an action plan by tomorrow. In the interim, he received a call from the lieutenant. He retreated to the conference room to speak with him privately.

I returned to my desk and sat down. Alone in the office area, I sensed a heavy weight in the air. It was filled with grief, sadness, and something else. Fear. Yes, fear of a serial killer whose vendetta had crossed the decades. We had to find this maniac before he succeeded in killing more of his targets.

Ryan came up to my desk minutes later, his expression strained. "I had a serious conversation with your Uncle Ted. He wanted confirmation that I'd protect you, no matter what."

"You already promised him you'd drive me to work and back home," I said.

"It's not enough."

"Is that your decision or my uncle's?"

With an unwavering look on his face, he leaned closer to me and said, "After that anonymous call you got today, Amber, and after what happened to Nadia's boyfriend, I'm not leaving your side for a second. And that's final."

What followed was a heated conversation between us. Ryan

persisted in extending his protection over me at all hours, and I stood my ground for independence. We finally agreed there was no other way he could ensure my safety while keeping his promise to Uncle Ted.

In essence, it meant Ryan was moving in with me on the weekend.

24

The DNA lab report from forensics flipped our world upside down the following morning. Contrary to our suspicions that Kenneth had fathered Susan Kendall's baby, tests revealed that the opposite was true. He was *not* the father.

"Do you realize what this means?" I said to Ryan. "As if things couldn't get more complicated."

"I'm considering other possibilities right now." He pointed to the two-page lab report in his hand. "First, Kenneth killed Susan because he knew she was pregnant, and it would have ruined his medical career. Second, if he knew she was pregnant and believed it was someone else's child, he could have felt betrayed and killed her out of anger."

"But Kenneth is a doctor. Think about that for a moment. What happened to 'First, do no harm'? I find it hard to accept that he would commit murder."

"Is that your psychic perception talking?"

"No."

"Do you honestly think Kenneth would have accepted a stranger's child as his own?"

I had an answer for that one. "Yes. He adopted three kids later on, didn't he?"

Ryan raised a forefinger in the air. "Good point. However, I maintain one thing. If Susan told Kenneth she was pregnant, and he believed it wasn't his child, he might have reacted in anger. It's a strong motive for murder. Lab tests indicate there were numerous stab wounds in Susan's body. It's a sign of rage."

"My perceptions confirmed it. The rage part, I mean."

"Right." He studied the first page of the report. "Furthermore, the opinion from forensics implies that the perp had experience in handling sharp objects." He glanced up at me. "A doctor knows the vulnerable areas in a body."

"Richard Kendall worked in construction and other similar trades," I pointed out. "Those jobs required the use of sharp tools too."

"On the subject of sharp objects, we can throw Bill Hardy into the mix. He must be an expert in handling kitchen knives."

"Let me add another likelihood," I said. "None of our three potential suspects killed Susan. Someone else did."

Ryan nodded slowly. "It could well be another probability." He flipped to the second page of the lab report. "Hold on here. Forensics did an analysis of the fingerprints on the ultrasound photo of the baby. They were a match with Kenneth's." His astonished expression said it all.

I almost jumped out of my chair. "Kenneth lied! He told us he hadn't seen the photo!"

"He's hiding something. That much is clear."

"We should meet with him again. He needs to know he's not the father."

Ryan reached for his phone. "I'll call his office to set up an appointment."

I waited while he spoke with the medical assistant. After our last meeting with the doctor, it wouldn't surprise me if he'd find an excuse not to grant us another visit.

"I see. Thank you." Ryan placed his phone on his desk. "The doctor is away at a conference and can't be reached."

I recalled parts of our previous conversation with Kenneth. "Do you remember how surprised he was to learn that Susan was pregnant? Even after he saw the ultrasound photo, he denied it and explained how they'd taken precautions. Then he said she would have told him if she was pregnant." I rubbed my right temple. "This is getting so complex. Why would Kenneth lie to us about having seen the photo?"

He rolled his chair over to my desk. "You're right. He probably lied to us...about everything. Whatever the reason for killing Susan, there's a huge chance he's our perp. He's not off our list yet."

Nadia's arrival at the unit triggered the next topic of conversation. She gave a little wave in our direction before sitting at her desk. With makeup and her hair in curls, she looked like her old self again.

"I spoke with Chris Farand, the officer who responded to the fatality involving Nadia's boyfriend the other night," Ryan whispered to me. "A blurred image of a light sedan appeared on a video from a local business surveillance camera. The lens was covered with frost, so no other details were available. The officer updated Nadia about it."

"One of our potential suspects must be involved," I said, keeping my voice low. "Who also happens to be our mystery caller."

"We'll interview each one again, aside from Richard Kendall, of course. He can hardly walk, let alone drive."

"The doctor is out of town, but Bill Hardy is available," I hinted.

"Okay. Let's pay him a visit. Now. Unannounced."

Bill Hardy's jaw dropped when he opened the door to his apartment. "What is it this time? Did I forget to pay my electricity bill?"

Ryan edged past him, leading the way inside. "Do you own a car?"

Bill left the door slightly open and within reach. "No, I don't."

"Have you leased a car recently?"

"No, I haven't."

"Where were you two nights ago?"

"Why? Did you discover another body?" he scoffed.

Ryan kept his cool. "You could say that."

Anger swept over Bill's face. "Unless you have a search warrant, you have no right to be here. I let you in out of politeness. Now get the hell out of here!" He took two steps toward the door and opened it wide.

Faced with no alternative, Ryan and I left. Our impromptu interview with Bill was the shortest meeting we'd had so far. If you could even call it a meeting.

On our way back to the car, Ryan joked, "That went over pretty well, didn't it?"

I smiled. "If it's any consolation, Bill was telling the truth."

"Which means we're back to square one."

"Not necessarily. Bill Hardy or Kenneth Cameron could have hired someone to do their dirty work for them."

"In that case, it's next to impossible to pin this week's hit-and-run crime on either of them."

"What if we're jumping to conclusions, Ryan? What if Nadia's boyfriend was killed by a drunk driver and it had nothing to do with Susan Kendall's case?" When he didn't answer, I continued my rant. "We should leave the car incident to Officer Chris Farand to investigate. After all, it is his case. Don't you think we have enough cases to solve?"

"True."

We rode back to the unit in silence. I couldn't read Ryan's

mind, but I wouldn't be surprised if he was wondering the same thing as me: Will we ever get a break in the three cold cases we were working on?

Back at the unit, Matt's heavy gait alerted us to his approach. He dropped a file on his desk and pulled up a chair close to mine.

Ryan strolled over to join us. "You have good news for us, Matt?"

"You bet I do." Matt sat down. "Remember Devon Hill, the guy who worked for Bill Hardy at the diner in Willowburg?"

"He was the assistant cook at The Easy Diner," I said.

"Exactly," Matt said. "I'm going to his place tomorrow evening to interview him."

"Where does he live?" Ryan asked him.

"In Montreal North. Up by the river."

"I'll go with you," Ryan said. "It's a tough area of town. Street gangs with guns."

Matt shook his head. "You don't have to. I can manage—"

"Don't even think about it."

Now it was "street gangs with guns" and the safety of my two colleagues. More situations to increase my angst.

25

———

Lieutenant Payton issued a directive the next morning: The unit needed to speed up the entry of paperwork details in almost eight hundred cold case files into the database.

"It will ultimately reduce the time we spend digging through shelves of boxes in response to requests for information coming from outside the unit," the lieutenant said. "It's urgent that all our police departments, like homicide, have access to the numerous files taking up space in our storage room. Other police forces across the country will benefit from access to our case data."

"Sir, I can assure you we're doing the best we can," Ryan said, defending the efforts of the team. "Numerous case reports were incomplete or needed interpreting by one of us before input."

"That's fine, but speed is of the essence," the lieutenant said. "Keep me informed of your progress." He returned to his office.

With their days spent on locating the whereabouts of witnesses for us, working on the police website, and handling incoming calls on the Info-Crime line, Nadia and Corey had barely made a dent in uploading information from the hundreds of bankers boxes stacked in the storage room. Ryan, Matt, and I had helped them by reviewing and clarifying details in the files when time permitted. We agreed we'd work extra hours today, even if it meant we'd get through a fraction of the files.

Early that evening, Matt interrupted my concentration when he stood up and tidied his desk. He cast a glance in Ryan's direction as he also rose from his chair.

"I'm telling you, Ryan, I'm okay with meeting Devon Hill on my own," Matt said, annoyance running through his voice as he shoved papers into his backpack. "He's my last witness anyway. He must have all kinds of information about Susan Kendall. We need a miracle statement from the guy, and I'm sure I can get it."

"Matt, I'm not questioning your capacity to get the info," Ryan said, slipping into his jacket. "The fact is that violent crime rates are off the charts where your witness lives, day or night. Street gang shootings there are common."

My nerves tingled. They were about to venture into a dangerous part of the city. Then again, those risks came with the job.

"Fine. Let's go." Matt grabbed his backpack and plodded off into the hall.

Ryan whispered to me, "We should be back in an hour or so. Wait for me and I'll drive you home."

After they left, I got a call from Aunt Elaine. "Are you at work, dear?"

I sensed uneasiness in her voice. "Yes. Is anything wrong?"

"Amber, now I don't want to alarm you. As you know, the images we get can be interpreted in different ways."

Uh-oh. She had one of her ominous insights again. Since we came from the same psychic lineage, it was an innate trait she shared with me. "What did you see, Aunt Elaine?"

"Well, I was looking out the window at the falling snow and had a vision of cracked glass suddenly exploding. I called your Uncle Ted and told him about it. He agreed I should warn you and Ryan to be careful driving home. The roads are slippery out there."

"Don't worry, Aunt Elaine. We're working late anyway." She didn't have to know that Ryan was off-site. She'd worry even more. "The snow crews will clean up the streets before we leave. Besides, we don't have far to drive."

"Amber, dear, can you do me a favor and call me when you get home?"

"I will."

At around eight o'clock, the sound of snowplows on the main street was music to our ears. Nadia and Corey had made progress in uploading a substantial number of files to the database. The lieutenant would be pleased. They packed it up and were escorted home by police cruisers.

I hadn't heard from Ryan yet. Half an hour later, my worry radar increased. I didn't want to call him in case he and Matt had extended their interview for one reason or another. I reviewed old case files for tomorrow's input, but my focus kept wandering.

What if they had run into trouble? After all, Ryan had emphasized the violent crime rates and street gangs in the area they were visiting.

The ringtone on my phone broke the silence. It was Ryan. My heart pounding, I swooped up the phone.

"Hi, Amber." The sound of Ryan's voice comforted me until he said, "There's been a delay. I need to hang around here a while longer."

I captured an image of spattered blood. Shivers ran down my spine. "Ryan, are you okay?"

"I-I can't talk right now," he stammered. "Can you drive home on your own?"

"You're scaring me. Are you sure you're all right?"

"Yes. It's just going to take a while longer to wrap things up here."

"Okay. See you later." I ended the call. Things were not all right.

After I confirmed that the off-site receptionist for the Info-Crime line was on duty, I picked up my handbag and left.

I trudged through mounds of snow in the parking lot behind the building and searched for my dark gray car. Finding it among a dozen unmarked police cars in various shades of gray wasn't an easy task, not to mention the extra layer of snow now blanketing them. I finally found my car and cleaned the snow off. My winter tires eased the short drive to the street.

The plows had passed, yet it was snowing hard again, and the roads were slushy. As was my habit, I often checked my rearview mirror to make sure I wasn't being followed. The side streets I took were dimly lit but there was hardly any traffic. Comforted that I'd be home within minutes, I relaxed and turned on the radio to listen to music.

A sudden chill enveloped me moments later. It wasn't the first time my spidery sense had warned me about danger.

I glanced at my rearview mirror. A light sedan was barely two car lengths behind me, but I couldn't determine the make or model of the vehicle due to the heavy snowfall.

I maintained my speed while keeping an eye on the sedan. Its headlights blinded me, then vanished as the driver accelerated and swiftly closed the distance between us.

I sped up but not fast enough. The sedan hit my car with a hard thud. The impact hurled me against the side window. The second impact thrust me into the steering wheel. I lost control and smashed into large stones decorating a front lawn.

The last thing I remembered was the sound of glass cracking, the inflated airbag walloping against my head, and then, darkness.

"It's a mild concussion."

The doctor's diagnosis didn't surprise me. The lump on the side of my head had been the preliminary indicator. The bruises on my face from the inflated airbag, another. Everything had happened so quickly that I only had hazy memories of the incident.

"Is it okay if I take her home now?" Ryan asked him.

"Yes," the doctor said. "If there's any sign that things are getting worse, come back to the hospital."

It was after midnight when Ryan drove me home. He didn't speak but occasionally glanced at me, as if he wanted to say something but couldn't.

He finally said, "What happened to you was my fault, Amber. I shouldn't have let you drive home alone."

"You're not to blame," I said. "No one could have known what was going to happen."

Ryan tightened his grip on the steering wheel. "It doesn't matter. I wasn't thinking. I should have requested a police escort for you."

I gently put a hand on his arm. "You don't have to worry about me. I'll be okay." My voice sounded weak, even to me. It was no doubt the effect of the sedative the doctor had given me.

"Is that the psychic part of you talking? Or are you trying to calm me down after the investigating officer told me how someone had tried to kill you?" He stared at me. "You do realize that someone hit your car with intent to seriously harm you, don't you?"

"Yes. I told the police officer who interviewed me what had happened."

"They called me when they brought you in. I was sick with worry." Ryan put his hand on mine and squeezed.

I squeezed back. "Stop worrying about me. When we get home, I'll tell you all about it."

"There's no rush. Right now, you need to rest."

The windshield on the passenger side was cracked and distorted my vision, so I couldn't see anything anyway. I closed my eyes and dozed off, puzzled as to why Ryan was driving my car and not his.

26

___

Recurring scenes from my car crash woke me up three times during the night. At one point, the dream was so vivid that I screamed and caused Ryan to bound from the bed. He thought an intruder had broken into the house. To make up for lost sleep, I slept in the next morning.

The weekend had arrived, yet Saturday brought me no respite. Aside from the car incident, other matters weighed heavily on my mind. The interviews with witnesses in Susan Kendall's case were wedged in my brain, as were questions that had produced no leads so far. I couldn't help but sense that Susan herself was screaming for a solution. Unfortunately, we weren't making any progress in finding her killer.

Ryan's presence in my home comforted me to an extent, although every time there was a knock at the door, my body tensed up. The first time, it was a delivery of products I'd ordered from a local store the other day and forgotten about. The second knock was a young boy asking if we needed our walkway shoveled.

Ryan handled the intrusions with more composure than I could have managed. I showed my gratitude by preparing a brunch Saturday noon. After we'd eaten, we moved to the living room with our cups of coffee and had a conversation about my "accident."

After he set his cup on the coffee table, Ryan took my hand in his. "I feel terrible about the other night. It was my job to protect you, and I failed. I'm so sorry, Amber."

"It wasn't your fault," I said. "I took the usual precautions, but it happened so fast." The reality of my almost fatal accident had begun to sink in. I blinked back the tears.

"What you experienced was terrifying. I promise I won't let anything like that happen to you again." He paused. "Our investigation of the cold cases triggered it. The murder of Nadia's boyfriend too. Our perp is showing signs that he's taking us seriously. It means we're getting close."

Fear mounted inside me. "Seriously enough to come after us personally. It means everyone at the unit is at risk."

Ryan reached for his coffee cup. "We'll take more precautions. We can't give him another opportunity to retaliate against any of us." He took a few sips.

"Does that mean we're going to interview our potential suspects again? Ask them where they were the night of my 'accident'?"

"Not at this time."

I mentally skimmed our list. "I'd eliminate Richard Kendall for obvious reasons. Aside from sounding like a parrot, I'll say this again. Even if Bill Hardy told us he doesn't own a car, he could have paid someone to commit a crime for him. The same thing goes for Kenneth Cameron. Money has no limit for him." I caught myself. I was venting, with anger, fear, and frustration forming a volcanic alliance. "Sorry. I didn't mean to—"

"It's okay, Amber." Ryan's tone was soothing. "You've been through a terrifying ordeal. The investigating officer will get back to me if they obtain any surveillance camera videos in the area. We'll take appropriate steps then."

I remembered another precarious incident. "How did your meeting go with Devon Hill last evening?"

"Hard to say. The guy is in his late sixties. He's a drug addict, so we can't take everything he says seriously. On the other hand, something he said could cast a different light on one of our three suspected individuals."

"Which one?"

"Bill Hardy."

"What did Devon say?"

Ryan drank more coffee. "When he was working at The Easy Diner, he admitted he was attracted to Susan but was reluctant to ask her out. He overheard part of her argument with Bill in the room behind the kitchen right before she quit."

"Oh!" My interest surged. "What did he hear?"

"Bits of conversation here and there. Something about money...supporting her. It was vague."

"Is that it?" I drank some coffee.

"That's all he overheard," Ryan said. "Something else happened at the diner soon afterward."

"What?"

"It was Christmas Eve, and people were pouring in. Dinner orders were piling up. Devon was furious when Bill said he had to go get provisions because the kitchen was running out of basic supplies. Devon had to hustle like crazy to get the orders filled."

"Does Devon remember what time Bill got back?"

"I asked him about that. He said he was busy and didn't notice the exact time. He said one minute Bill was gone, the next he was back in the kitchen. Bill surprised him by taking out the garbage while Devon cooked the meals."

"Was that rare? Taking out the garbage?"

Ryan nodded. "Like you, my radar went up, and I asked him that exact question. Instead of yelling at Devon to take out the garbage like he usually did, Bill took it out himself. It made me question if he was trying to hide something."

"Like a knife?" I said with sarcasm.

"Now wouldn't that be convenient," he said. "No, Devon assumed Bill was being kind for a change, seeing that it was the Christmas season. He must have had second thoughts the next day when Susan's body was discovered."

"Did Devon say if he suspected Bill was involved with her murder?"

"Not in so many words. He did say that Bill had a lot of control over the staff. As a younger employee, Devon was afraid of him. He put aside that fear the next day when he heard about Susan's murder. He was curious and wanted to go check the garbage that Bill had dumped outside."

My pulse increased. "Did he?"

"No, but I wish he had," Ryan said. "Days later, Devon quit his job at the diner and went to work at a fast-food restaurant in Trimville. And we know what happened there."

"Michelle Roy was stabbed to death and dumped among garbage bags behind the restaurant. Devon discovered her body."

A tiny frown gathered between Ryan's eyes. "You should have seen Devon. The guy is hooked on drugs and has that glazed, faraway look in his eyes. He said he's depressed about where he's at in his life. He kept saying how he wished he could have done something good for a change."

I set my coffee cup aside. "That's so sad. What about accessing rehab facilities?"

"He tried but can't get in," Ryan said. "There's a waiting list a mile long. The dump of an apartment he's living in doesn't help either. Drug addicts slumped in the hallways of the building...needles discarded everywhere..."

"How does he survive? I mean, he's not working. Where does he get the money?"

"He told me he has friends he does favors for. Sounds to me like he could be dealing as well as using."

"It makes you wonder what happened to people like Devon to end up in a situation like that."

"Two things. Bad luck and hanging out with the wrong crowd." Ryan was undeniably speaking from his experience in homicide.

"Getting back to Bill Hardy," I said, "we agree that he had the means and opportunity to commit murder. He remains a potential suspect, right?"

"Even if we try to link Bill to Susan's murder, we don't have much in the way of motive or physical evidence. We have more work to do on these cases. Time is running out."

I assumed he was referring to the approaching Christmas holidays or that we needed to solve more cold cases to meet the lieutenant's mandate. Or both.

Another memory surfaced. "When you were with Matt the other night and you called me, you mentioned a delay," I said. "What happened?"

Ryan passed a hand through his hair. "When we walked out of Devon's place, a surprise was waiting for us outside."

"What?"

"We'd noticed two gang members when we parked the car in front of the apartment building. They must have recognized that the unmarked car belonged to cops. When we went back to the car, we found the front windshield cracked on the passenger side. It looked as if someone had taken a baseball bat to it."

It explained the damaged windshield when Ryan drove me home from the hospital. It was *his* car we were riding in, not mine!

"How did you know they were gang members?" I asked him.

"The organized crime unit sends us updates on violent gang involvement in crimes like car theft, fraud, and murder. We get info on gang insignia, their habits, and the places they frequent. Matt and I noticed the insignia on their jackets. They're not fans of the police."

I imagined another scenario. "What if they weren't responsible for the damage to your car? What if our anonymous caller sent you a warning?"

"The police are reviewing surveillance videos in the area," Ryan said. "We'll find out more soon enough." He fixed me with a serious look. "Amber, I want you to know that as soon as I got the call about your accident, I drove straight to the hospital."

"I don't doubt it. Did Matt go with you?"

"He had no choice. I was driving." He smiled. "A cruiser picked him up at the hospital and drove him back to the station to get his car."

Then I remembered. "What about my car? How damaged was it?"

"I had it towed. It'll be in the repair shop for a while."

I estimated the bill would be huge and sighed.

"Don't worry," Ryan said. "Since the incident occurred when you were on your way home from work, the unit will cover the expenses. Approval came from higher up." He winked.

"Uncle Ted? I mean, Chief Tremblay?"

"The one and only. He called while you were sleeping this morning."

"I'll call him back right now." I stopped. "Wait. You answered my phone?"

"You left it in the kitchen last night. It rang this morning, and I saw his name. Uncle Ted."

I let out a sigh of relief. "So, he doesn't know you moved in with me. I mean, temporarily."

"No, he doesn't," Ryan said. "We're covered."

After I called Uncle Ted and thanked him for covering my car expenses, he said, "We want to do whatever we can to keep you safe, Amber."

Aunt Elaine was relieved that I was okay and that her premonition had resulted in a satisfactory outcome. Like me, she wasn't perfect when it came to deciphering the images she perceived. The passage of time often revealed the truth behind our insights, and the horrors they sometimes brought.

27

Nicole called me late Sunday morning and asked if we were getting together in the afternoon. It was my turn to invite her over.

I didn't mention the car crash. It would have opened a Pandora's box of questions from my best, but inquisitive, friend. I made up an excuse instead. I told her I wasn't feeling well, which was somewhat true. She understood and agreed to get together another weekend.

Enjoying time alone with Ryan was what I needed right now. I appreciated his calm demeanor and the way he spent his weekends at a relaxed pace. This Sunday was especially quiet yet exciting. We were putting up the Christmas tree!

Ryan made a trip to his apartment to pick up clean clothes for the week. He also brought over his Christmas decorations. Combined with mine and the ones I inherited from my parents, we had plenty to choose from. I prepared mugs of hot chocolate while we sorted through glittery tree ornaments, velvet ribbons, and strings of beads to dress up the real Fraser fir tree he'd purchased.

I wasn't surprised when Ryan brought up the topic of moving in together. He's raised it a couple of times before.

"We're either at your place or mine," he said. "Don't you think living together would be beneficial to both of us?"

I answered with hesitancy. "It might not work. What about the office rules? What if someone found out about us? It would mean that we couldn't work together anymore. One of us would have to give up our jobs. The cold case investigations are so important to both of us."

"I understand the implications. I'd ask for a transfer to another area. I could go back to homicide."

"No way," I insisted. "The cold case unit is yours. You earned it. I would quit first."

Ryan's tone was firm. "They wouldn't allow it."

"*They?*" I repeated. "You mean my uncle."

"He wouldn't go for it. You're an asset to the unit."

Our argument went back and forth for several more rounds until I put an end to it. "Let's forget about work and enjoy the rest of this weekend. Okay?"

"Excellent idea," Ryan said. "Let's wrap this up and watch a movie."

We'd finished decorating the tree and putting away the left-over ornaments when he received an urgent message on his phone.

"It's from the night-shift operator at the main switchboard," he said, his expression uneasy. "They received a bomb threat at Montreal police headquarters and called in the ERT."

"The ERT?"

"The Montreal Emergency Response Team. It's a specialized tactical unit that deals with high-risk interventions. They're preparing to enter the building."

"Ryan, that building has nine floors."

"The ERT is experienced in this type of situation." He elaborated. "The team will use specialized equipment to sweep the building for explosives or hazardous materials. It'll take a while. They'll communicate the results after they're done."

My breath stuck in my throat. Did the bomb threat come from the same person who had called the Info-Crime line and threatened me? The same person who had killed Nadia's boyfriend and rammed into my car?

After these latest incidents, I had a horrible feeling that Lieutenant Payton would be uneasy about keeping me on staff at the unit. The string of anonymous calls had targeted me from the start and put everyone else I worked with at risk.

My heart grew heavy with angst. My presence at the unit spelled bad news. Was this the end of my career?

We had a sleepless night while we waited for the ERT results. By five o'clock Monday morning, the team had determined the bomb threat was a hoax. An all-clear message was sent to police departments located in the building.

Everyone in the unit had received the all-clear message, yet employees returned to work with anxious expressions. Burdened with lingering insecurity, they searched inside their desks and cabinets, as if something dangerous might have been overlooked. To reassure the staff they were safe, Lieutenant Payton informed them that uniformed patrols were now in place to safeguard the premises.

For Ryan and me, it was business as usual. We drove out for an impromptu meeting with Dr. Kenneth Cameron. His medical receptionist claimed we needed an appointment, but with the doctor's door ajar and Kenneth noticing our arrival, Ryan led the way in.

"We have important news, Dr. Cameron," Ryan said, shutting the door behind us.

"Please, sit down." Kenneth gestured toward the two chairs facing his desk, then took a seat opposite us.

Ryan was direct. "We received the DNA results for Susan Kendall's unborn child. You're not the father."

Kenneth blinked hard. "I'm not surprised," he said, unperturbed. "After I got married, I went through a round of tests. They indicated I was sterile. That's why my wife and I adopted three children."

"Did you know about your medical condition when you met Susan?"

Kenneth stared at him. "How could I have known? Like I told you at our last meeting, we took precautions."

I refused to back down. "Aren't you the least bit concerned that the baby wasn't yours?"

Kenneth fixed his gaze on me. "Like I said, I believed that Susan was faithful to me, so I accepted that it was my baby. What was important was that Susan wanted to marry me, no matter what. Besides, I was her single ticket out of town."

I didn't buy his snarky, egotistical response. "She could have left town on her own."

"Not without my generous help." He dismissed my claim with a wave of his hand.

I couldn't believe what I was hearing. How bombastic!

Ryan jumped in before I let loose and told Kenneth exactly what I was thinking. "What generous help are you referring to?"

"I was Susan's salvation," Kenneth said, raising his chin with pride, "not only from a cruel father but also from that horrendous owner of the diner where she worked."

"Bill Hardy?"

"Yes. There wasn't a day when Susan didn't have to repel his advances. So told me other waitresses quit because of their fatigue fighting him off and his stinginess with their pay." Kenneth gathered the folders on his desk into a neat pile. It was a sign that our time with him was almost up.

Ryan must have sensed it too because he changed the subject. "We have reason to believe that your family disapproved of your marriage to Susan. Rich man marries poor small-town girl."

"Rumors," Kenneth said. "Just rumors."

"The information came from reliable sources."

Kenneth scowled. "Sergeant, I dislike the fact you're implicating my parents in your investigation. They died years ago. Let them rest in peace." He stood up. "If you'll excuse me, I have patients to see."

Ryan rose to his feet, but I wasn't finished.

"One more thing," I said, standing up. "You lied to us about not having seen the ultrasound photo of Susan's baby. Forensics found your fingerprints on it."

Kenneth gaped at me, then picked up the folders, stalling for a reply. "Okay. I admit that Susan showed me the ultrasound photo of the baby. I lied to you because otherwise you'd label me as a suspect. You'd blame me for her murder, say that I wanted to get rid of her to pursue a medical career, or you'd invent some other ridiculous idea."

"We haven't completed our investigation yet," Ryan said in a firm tone.

Kenneth moved to the door and opened it. "If you have any more questions, feel free to call me."

Driving back to the unit, Ryan said, "Talk about a reversal! Kenneth's admission that he lied to us about the ultrasound photo makes me wonder what else he lied about. Did you pick up any insights from him, Amber?"

"Exactly what you observed," I said. "He wasn't surprised when we told him it wasn't his baby. He lied to us because he thought it could work against him and incriminate him in Susan's murder."

"Right."

"One thing is clear," I said. "Kenneth wants to put this part of his past behind him. He answers our questions out of forced politeness, but he's annoyed that we continue to hound him about the case."

"Bottom line?"

I voiced my opinion, even though I was sure Ryan would disagree with me. "Despite my insights, I'm not getting any violent vibes from Kenneth. I can't say for certain that he murdered Susan."

Ryan alleged otherwise. "A killer will tell the cops what they want to hear. Here's how I see it. The doctor admitted he lied to us about the ultrasound photo. He knew about Susan's pregnancy all along. If he believed it would interfere with his career or tarnish his family's reputation, he had the motive, means, and opportunity to kill her. He stays on our list of potential suspects."

28

On our return to the unit, Ryan and I sat down with Matt to discuss the two cases he'd been working on. We'd expected he'd have an update for victims Michelle Roy and Pamela Cooper.

"Their pages on the police website are up and running now," Matt said, hope filtering through his voice. "All we need are leads to come in through the Info-Crime line."

"Any news from forensics?" Ryan asked him.

"I got their lab report minutes ago." He handed it to Ryan. "There are no DNA or fingerprint matches between the trace evidence in these two cases nor when compared with those in Susan Kendall's case."

Ryan studied the report. "Another dead end."

"Maybe we should be looking for two killers," Matt said.

"I don't agree," I said. "The MO is similar in all three cases. My insights tell me it's the same killer."

"We can't argue with that." Ryan handed the lab report back to Matt.

"What about a copycat killer?" Matt asked.

"Unlikely," Ryan said. "The evidence at the crime scenes has never been made public."

"Which means we can't put the stuff about the matches up on the website." Matt slid the report into a file.

"It would encourage anybody who wanted to admit to the crime—even though they didn't do it—to come forward," Ryan said. "Like a copycat." He gave Matt a knowing look.

"Point taken," Matt said.

"Some people will do anything for their fifteen minutes of fame," I said.

"If we're searching for the same perp," Matt said, "he got a lot wiser after he killed Susan. He left no comparable trace evidence with his two subsequent victims, Michelle and Pamela. No hair, fibers, fingerprints, you name it."

I brought up a related theory. "Ryan, what if those two women were killed somewhere else, like in another town?"

"And their bodies dumped in a different location," Matt said, completing my theory.

"It's a possibility, but we need to find another common denominator to link all three cases," Ryan said. "Let's brainstorm. I'll start. We have three female victims who lived in different towns. We also have three persons of interest with plausible motives to commit murder."

I jumped in. "Because of the distance between towns, we can assume the killer traveled as a requirement of his job."

"Or he could be a drifter," Matt suggested.

"Okay," Ryan said. "Let's apply these theories to the information we have on hand about our plausible suspects, including the evidence."

"Kenneth Cameron traveled to other towns for the family strawberry business before he left for medical school," I said. "Richard Kendall traveled to work on construction and other projects."

"Bill Hardy sold his diner and worked at restaurants in other places," Matt said.

"As for the matches left at the crime scene," I said, "our three men could have been smokers."

"Or still are," Matt added.

"Right," Ryan said. "One more thing. We have the doctor's DNA on file. We don't have tangible evidence against the other two guys on our list. We need to obtain fingerprints and DNA samples from them so forensics can compare them to whatever trace evidence is on the three sets of burnt matches."

His request astonished me. "You want to ask Susan's father for his DNA? I doubt he'd agree to give us a sample." Then I remembered. "Wait. We have the letter Lisa sent him. That's good enough, isn't it?"

"You bet." Ryan smiled. "Richard's DNA and fingerprints are on that letter. Based on Lisa's statement, he could have gone into town after he overheard her phone conversation with Susan. He knew exactly where and when Susan was supposed to meet Kenneth. I'll send Lisa's letter to forensics to see if there's a match with the evidence on hand."

"Smart move," Matt said with an appreciative nod.

The idea that a father would murder his own daughter gave me shivers. And doubts. "If you both think Richard had a strong motive to kill his daughter, what would be his motive to kill the other two women?"

The puzzled expression on Matt's face was revealing. He didn't know what to say.

"The mindset of a serial killer is complex," Ryan said. "They view their murders as a vocation, as hard work. In our three cases, I believe it's about power and control. Certain victims trigger the killer's response."

"What would the trigger be?" Matt asked him.

"It's a theory, but maybe Richard wanted a soft-hearted woman to replace the wife and daughters he lost. When it didn't work out for him, he disposed of them."

"Like garbage," Matt said, grimacing. "What a sicko."

I repressed my disgust and moved on to another suspect.

"What about Bill Hardy, the owner of the diner? We need his fingerprints."

"Then I'd say he merits another visit," Ryan said.

Matt wasn't convinced. "He's a tough guy. He'll refuse to give us a DNA sample. He lives in an apartment block, so we have no access to his garbage to search for something with his DNA on it."

"We can follow him around town to get it," Ryan said. "What do you say, Amber?"

"We?" I repeated. "Like you and me?"

"Yes, you and me," Ryan said. "We'll be less noticeable if we work as a couple. We can disguise ourselves and tail Bill on foot when he leaves his apartment. We have an opportunity to do that since he takes his dog out a few times a day."

"I guess I'm out of the picture on that little escapade," Matt said, sounding dejected. "Ryan, I've interviewed all my witnesses. What do you want me to do in the meantime?"

"Create a timeline for our three potential suspects and pin it to the crazy wall over there." Ryan gestured toward the evidence board. "Our concentration will be on which one could have traveled to the towns where the bodies of Michelle Roy and Pamela Cooper were found. The emphasis is on the suspect's place of residence and the distance and time involved to travel to each of those towns."

My phone buzzed and I answered.

It was Jennifer Sarto. "I've been away the last while visiting relatives. What can I do for you, Amber?" When I asked if she could search her school photos for a student named Ernie, she said, "I'd like to help you, but I don't have any photos of male students. You see, boys and girls weren't integrated in the same classrooms back then. I only taught the girls."

"Do you know who taught the boys?"

"Yes. It was Mr. Finch. He passed away ten years ago."

I thanked her and ended the call.

Another dead end.

At least the weather was promising. With milder temperatures in the forecast, it was the perfect day for a stroll. Frost glistened on tree branches, and icicles shone in the sun. But the covert operation that Ryan and I were about to launch was far from a pleasure trip.

I donned a blonde wig and sunglasses as part of my disguise. Ryan wore a baseball cap and sunglasses. We hunkered down in the car on the street not far from Bill Hardy's apartment building and waited. An hour later, he walked out with his golden retriever on a leash.

Ryan and I stepped out of the car and followed a safe distance behind him. We tailed him along the sidewalk and around a corner toward the park. The sunny afternoon had drawn many people out today. It made it easier for us to survey Bill while mingling among pedestrians who ambled along the path through the park.

Fifteen minutes later, Bill stopped and sat down on a bench, his dog resting at his feet. He pulled out a pair of eyeglasses and a magazine from inside his winter coat. He slowly flipped through the pages.

"He's not wearing gloves," Ryan pointed out.

"Excellent for fingerprints," I said. "All the more reason I hope he trashes the magazine before he gets home."

Ryan and I edged closer to where Bill was sitting. We stopped across the path from him and took advantage of the small groups of pedestrians to mask our presence. I leaned against a tree with my back to Bill. Ryan aimed his phone at me and took a photo, making sure to include Bill in the background of the shot. A photo enlargement would later confirm that Bill undeniably had the magazine in his possession.

"He looked in our direction," Ryan said, nestling closer to me to hide his face. "We can't stay here. Let's move to that clump of bushes on the left." He put his arm around my shoulder as we stepped farther away. From our hiding spot behind the bushes, we had a clear view of Bill, but he couldn't see us.

Fifteen more minutes went by. Bill put away his eyeglasses, then lit a cigarette. He rolled up the magazine and led his dog down the path toward his apartment building.

Ryan and I followed, hand in hand. Should Bill happen to glance over his shoulder, we wanted him to believe we were young lovers out on a stroll on a warmer than usual winter afternoon.

Every time Bill approached a wastebasket, I didn't dare blink. I didn't want to miss seeing him throw out his cigarette butt or the magazine that might have his DNA and fingerprints on it. But he passed two trash cans without stopping.

Our surveillance paid off soon enough. Bill tossed the magazine into a municipal garbage bin on the street. He dropped the cigarette butt and stubbed it out with his boot, then kept on walking.

We waited until he had turned the corner and was out of sight, then we raced to the bin. Excitement rose inside me as the success of our stakeout dawned upon me.

Evidence bag at the ready, Ryan slipped his gloved hand into the bin and retrieved the magazine that Bill had discarded. For good measure, he scooped up the crushed cigarette butt and dropped it into another evidence bag. Smiling, he said, "We did it. Let's get this evidence to forensics ASAP."

29

———

Ryan received a report the next morning from the police officer who had investigated my car crash. "Sorry, Amber. There were no cameras operating in the area where the crash occurred. However, they recovered a portion of the headlight belonging to the other vehicle and are attempting to track it down."

"That's encouraging news," I said, then turned around at the sound of approaching footsteps.

Lieutenant Payton's rapid stride in our direction didn't bode well. "Sergeant Baxter, I'd like to speak with you and Amber in my office right now." His tone was abrupt and loud enough for everyone else in the unit to take notice.

"Yes, sir." Ryan stood up and slipped into his jacket.

I jumped to my feet. The lieutenant's disturbing energy this early in the day sent quivers down my spine. Stunned stares from the other employees accentuated my qualms.

As we sat down in the lieutenant's glass-paneled office, I noticed the horizontal blinds were shut. Not a good sign.

The lieutenant cleared his throat. "As you know, our policy is to ensure the utmost safety and confidence in the day-to-day undertakings at the unit. Although the recent bomb threat was a hoax, extra uniforms are patrolling the area as a temporary measure today. It goes without saying that our security precautions extend to the staff in this building. To Amber, in particular." His eyes darted to me.

"Excuse me, sir," Ryan said. "You're not implying that the bomb scare was due to Amber's investigative work here, are you?"

"No, I'm not." The lieutenant observed me. "However, it's come to my attention that the chatter about your abilities, Amber, has broadened to areas that can influence public perception of how law enforcement operates at the unit."

"Sir, can you be more specific?" Ryan asked.

The lieutenant didn't have to. This was the moment I'd dreaded. To borrow an ominous phrase, it could signal the final nail in the coffin as far as my job at the unit was concerned.

"I'll be blunt," the lieutenant said. "A reporter called and asked for an interview with the 'psychic employee' who worked for us here." He raised his fingers to form air quotes.

It was the bombshell I'd anticipated!

The lieutenant continued. "Before either of you say something—and I can appreciate that you're prepared to defend your position—allow me to continue. After giving the matter serious consideration, Amber, I've decided to take you off the cases you're currently investigating. This is for your own safety and that of the unit, if not the entire division. The suspension period will depend on how successful we'll be in containing the...um...gossip. Any questions?"

I fought back the tears. I refused to show weakness at a time like this. "Lieutenant, we've gathered important evidence that can help solve three cold cases. I'd appreciate the opportunity to continue this work."

Ryan added his support. "Sir, each team member has gone beyond their job duties to ensure the success of the unit. Amber's ability to decipher evidence has assisted us immensely. The unity of the team is instrumental to solving cold cases."

"I commend the team's efforts," the lieutenant said. "My decision is based on one thing alone: to protect the integrity of the unit." He stood up. "That's all I have to say about the matter."

As Ryan and I stepped out of the lieutenant's office, Nadia and Corey looked up from their desks. Their puzzled expressions indicated they had questions for us but were afraid to voice them. I couldn't blame them. The lieutenant rarely spoke to us in his office behind closed doors, let alone with the blinds drawn.

Ryan whispered to me, "Let's go get a coffee." We detoured to the kitchen.

I watched as he filled two mugs. "How can this be happening, Ryan? We've come so far in narrowing down the potential killers in our three cases. How can I give it all up now based on a reporter chasing a story?"

"Reporters aren't your enemy. The bad guys are."

"I understand, but they're giving me a hard time all the same."

"Don't worry. I have an idea." He whispered the details of his strategic plan.

"Are you serious?" I stared at him. "What if the lieutenant takes offense? What if he fires the whole team?"

"He can't and he won't," Ryan said, sounding confident. "The lieutenant is experiencing a knee-jerk reaction. If we don't respond to inquiries from reporters, I'm convinced they'll lose interest, and the gossip about your abilities will stop. What do you think?"

I managed a smile. "Okay. It's worth a try."

Ryan gathered the team in the conference room to share the news about my temporary suspension. Their reactions astonished me.

"The lieutenant can't do that!" Matt said. "We're so close to solving these three cases. Besides, we'd be understaffed without Amber."

Nadia voiced similar words of support. "Ryan, did you tell the lieutenant how Amber gets special insights into the nature of Info-Crime callers? We can't afford to lose her."

"Amber is helping us to decipher a load of scribbled hand-written notes in the case files," Corey added. "The lieutenant gave us a deadline. It'll take more time to hire and train someone else to replace her."

What could have been construed as a defiant group, Ryan and my other coworkers knocked at the lieutenant's office door. He let them in.

I waited at my desk. With the door and blinds closed in the lieutenant's office, I had no idea what was happening in there.

I entertained the idea of calling Uncle Ted or Aunt Elaine to discuss the situation, but it would make things worse. The lieutenant wouldn't appreciate my going over his head either. No, using my connection to the chief of police was definitely not a proper approach. I had to stand on my own two feet.

The final decision was up to Lieutenant Payton now. I braced myself for whatever the future would throw my way.

Ten minutes went by, then fifteen. Was the length of time a good sign? I couldn't work. The suspense was killing me!

The door to the lieutenant's office opened and my support group stepped out. Nadia and Corey glimpsed in my direction before they hurried to their desks. I didn't pick up any negative vibes, so that was a relief.

Matt came out next. He whizzed by me and gave me a thumbs-up before sitting at his desk.

Ryan was the last to exit the lieutenant's office. He approached me, smiling. "We did it. The lieutenant reconsidered his decision. You're staying on."

Relief swept over me. "Fantastic! How did you manage it?"

"Aside from what we discussed and along with everyone

else's support," he whispered, "Nadia came out with the best argument for keeping you on."

"What did she say?"

"She mentioned that Christmas was two weeks away. She told the lieutenant it was cruel to suspend you at this special time of the year."

"She did?" I turned to look at her and smiled. She was speaking into her headset but caught my eye and gave me a little wave.

Lieutenant Payton stepped out of his office and strode toward us at a steady clip. He came up to me and said, "Amber, I assume you already heard the news."

"Yes," I said. "Thank you."

"Sergeant Baxter and the team spoke highly of you. I'll hold off on the suspension for now and see how it goes." He gave me a brief smile, then turned to Ryan. "I'm off to a security briefing. You know how to reach me." He walked out.

With the team back at work, I exhaled, releasing pent-up tension. Thanks to the full backing of my colleagues, I was still here.

But for how much longer?

30

———————

R yan received a report from the police officer who investigated the damage to his car windshield last week. No surveillance camera footage of the incident had been available, nor was the officer able to obtain any viable witness reports.

"From what you told me about the area," I said to Ryan, "I'm not surprised that anyone who witnessed the vandalism would be afraid to talk."

Matt added, "Those guys had probably worn balaclavas to hide their faces anyway." He reached for his phone to answer a call.

"Whoever did it must be having a good laugh," Ryan said, then leafed through a file on his desk.

My phone buzzed. It was Nadia. "Sorry, Amber, would you mind if I transferred a call on the Info-Crime line to you? I'm already on another call."

Matt was having a hushed conversation on the phone. I caught the gist of a discussion with his ex-wife about his kids and after-school activities. Ryan was busy entering information on his computer. "Okay, I'll take the call."

After I answered, a disguised voice boomed from the other end of the line. "You think you're so smart, all of you."

That thundering voice! My pulse quickened, but I tried to stay calm and objective. "Are you calling regarding a particular case?"

"I have news for you," the voice said. "You won't find me. Remember this: In order to give light, one must first burn."

The line went dead.

I stood up, my legs wobbly. "Ryan! It's the same caller."

He jumped to his feet. "Are you sure?"

I trembled involuntarily. "Y-yes."

Matt cut short his conversation on the phone and drew closer. "What's up?"

"I got the same caller as the other day," I said. "The one who talked about burning."

Ryan listened to the recorded call. "He must be referring to the burnt matches he left at the scene of the crime. It's his way of admitting he killed those women. This is our perp."

Matt brought a dose of reality into the conversation. "And all this time, I thought one of our three potential suspects might have had personal reasons to murder the women."

"Personal in a way that only *they* can justify," Ryan said. "They're using the burnt matches as a symbol of their retribution."

Laura had said something similar, that the matches could represent the killer's revenge and anger toward the victims. But why? I'd have to ask her at my next visit.

Ryan gestured toward the evidence board on a wall bordering the office. "Matt, show us what you have on the crazy wall so far."

After we moved to the evidence board, Matt pointed to a name. "Let's start with Richard Kendall. He held jobs in construction and transport and had to drive to different work sites. Chances are they weren't far away because Lisa said she cooked dinner for him every night."

"According to Lisa," I said, "Richard overheard her phone call with Susan. He knew she was meeting Kenneth near the flower shop that day. Kenneth was the only other person who knew the time and place of their meeting. It would eliminate Bill Hardy."

"Unless Bill followed her," Ryan said. "Devon Hill, the assistant cook, implied as much. Bill could have used his last-minute trip to the grocers as a convenient excuse."

"Speaking of Bill Hardy," Matt said, pointing to his name on the board, "he sold the diner right after New Year's Day. He worked as a temporary cook at other diners in nearby towns afterward. Not much income there. I'd say he lived mainly off the money from the sale of the diner."

I studied the lines connecting Bill Hardy's trajectory to different towns. "He did a fair bit of traveling." The name of a familiar town stood out. "Cedarberry. It's the same town where Pamela Cooper's body was discovered. When did he work there?"

"I think it was shortly after he sold the diner."

Ryan pressed his lips together. "He could be a blip on our radar."

"Let me check." Matt walked back to his desk and picked up the file. "According to former investigators, Bill's name had come up in connection with Susan's case during the same period. They definitely had their eyes on him. They tracked him down and interviewed him in Cedarberry. He had an alibi for the night Pamela Cooper was killed. He was working at a local diner that day and late into the night."

"It doesn't mean anything," I said, amusement in the works. "He could have left to buy supplies, and no one would have noticed."

Ryan's eyes twinkled and he smiled. "Okay, Amber, I get the sarcasm. Who's next, Matt?"

Matt walked back to the evidence board. "Next, we have Dr. Kenneth Cameron. He worked in sales at his family's strawberry business for a few months. It was right after Susan's death. He traveled to meet clients in nearby towns. And yes, it included Cedarberry."

"Similar timelines and distances for each of these men," Ryan noted.

"I don't want to put a damper on the work we've been doing," I said, "but I have a problem with all of this." I waved toward the evidence board.

"What's wrong?" Matt asked.

"We can't prove that any of our three suspects is guilty. Our theories make sense, but we have no physical proof to link any of these men to the murders."

"Amber, you're beginning to sound like Ryan," Matt said, chuckling. "I think you guys hang around together too much."

I held back a giggle. If he only knew the truth!

"Amber, you're right about the lack of physical proof," Ryan said. "We need more of it to solve these cases. Otherwise, our jobs at the unit are doomed." He motioned toward the evidence board and stayed on course. "We know that each of these three men played a role in Susan's life. It's not a fluke that two other murders with identical MOs occurred in such rapid succession after hers and within close proximity. The bottom line is that all three men had the motive, means, and opportunity to kill Susan. Similarly, we need to prove who the real perp is based on his connection to all three victims."

"Wait." Matt raised a hand in the air. "Let's not forget one thing. The murders in each of the three towns were one-offs. If you ask me, the perp moved to another location after he killed these victims."

"Okay." Ryan studied the board. "The doctor relocated to Montreal months later. Lisa eventually placed her father in a long-term care home in a Montreal suburb. Bill Hardy settled in Montreal as well."

I needed to voice my doubts about Kenneth Cameron again.

"No matter what you say, Ryan, I find it hard to accept that a doctor could turn into a serial killer."

"Serial killers span the range of occupations," he said. "You'll find them working in careers you least expect, like caregivers."

"Speaking of caregivers," Matt said, "I once investigated a homicide case involving a hospital nurse. She'd been adding morphine to the drip tubes connected to patients. Can you imagine?"

"It proves my point," Ryan said. "You got anything else, Matt?"

"I have nothing more to add," Matt said. His phone signaled an incoming call. "It's the Info-Crime line." He answered. Since we'd been getting threatening calls lately, Ryan and I stood by and listened in.

After a brief conversation, Matt ended the call, his eyes bulging with surprise. "You won't believe this. The caller wants to talk to me in person. He saw the website pages for Michelle Roy and Pamela Cooper. He claims he met them years ago at a pub and dated them. He said he might be able to describe their killer."

31

"In order to give light, one must first burn."

The quote from the anonymous caller on the Info-Crime line yesterday intrigued me and kept me awake half the night. Because of my trust in Laura as a close friend and psychologist, I planned to meet with her again. I needed an expert interpretation of the mysterious quote.

Ryan and two other officers in homicide were attending a course the next morning. His colleagues offered to give him a ride to the downtown location. Since my car was at the auto shop for repairs, and the damaged windshield on Ryan's car had been replaced, I asked if he'd lend me his car. He agreed with reluctance.

I visited Laura before my shift at the unit. Sitting across from her desk, I brought her up to date on the three cold cases we were currently investigating.

"The similar elements in each of them remind me even more of 'The Little Match Girl' by Hans Christian Andersen," I said.

A spark lit up Laura's eyes. "Ah, yes. You mentioned that

particular fairy tale during your last visit here. You say you now have *three* such cases?"

"Yes. Each of our three victims was a young, working woman who lived in a small town. Burnt matches were left at each crime scene. The first woman was killed during a snowstorm on Christmas Eve. The other two women, in different locations weeks later."

"I see."

"There's something I need your help with, Laura. An anonymous caller to the Info-Crime line, maybe the killer, recited this quote: 'In order to give light, one must first burn.' Any idea what it means?"

She steepled her fingers. "It's a variation of a citation by Victor Frankl. 'What is to give light must endure burning.'"

"Who's Victor Frankl?"

"He was an Austrian neurologist, psychologist, and philosopher who lived in the 1900s. He believed that an individual is the one responsible for deciding the meaning of their life. To attain that meaning, the individual must experience suffering."

"Could the killer be using that quote to imply he makes his victims suffer?"

"It's quite possible he discovered the quote and used it to suit his purposes." Laura leaned back in her chair. "If we compare what is portrayed in the fairy tale, the burnt matches in your cases can symbolize hope to the killer versus the hopelessness of a frigid winter."

"How?"

"As we discussed the last time, the killer sees himself as a savior, a symbol of hope, a liberator of his victims." She paused. "Here's another quote: 'Darkness fades but hope remains.' When we experience troubling times, we bond to the tiniest ray of promise. In the killer's mind, he is removing his victim from darkness and giving her hope."

"I can understand the premise, but I have a hard time

accepting that theory alone as a motive for murder. At my last visit here, you mentioned a more concrete motive, like revenge."

Laura nodded. "You're right. Acting as a savior to his victims may not be the killer's sole motive for murder. Let me explain." She leaned forward. "In your first victim's case, she quit her job on Christmas Eve and left her employer understaffed. Correct?"

"Yes, and it was extremely busy," I said.

"It's feasible that the killer was seeking retaliation for a perceived wrong. Although her cruel death would appear to be an extreme form of payback for abruptly leaving her job, one can't fully understand what goes on in a killer's mind."

Again, Ryan had said something similar. "What kind of traits should I look for in a suspect?"

"In relation to the fairy-tale premise," she said, "let's remember that the killer perceives the murder as a hopeful act of liberation on his part. He might not exhibit what we would consider deviant traits. Here's where the psychology can get more complicated. Perhaps in his youth, he struggled to free himself from being a target of bullying or from an overbearing adult. As an adult, he found strength in exercising his power over people he considered weaker than him, like trusting young women. He then set out to liberate them."

That description easily applied to each of our three suspects. Richard Kendall and his physical abuse of women. Bill Hardy and his domination over his female employees. Kenneth Cameron, who initially denied knowing about Susan's pregnancy and allegedly killed her or abandoned her.

I made another connection. "In the past, we discussed other cases where the killers had a fondness for fairy tales. Because of their beliefs, they made their victims suffer."

Laura fingered two pens on her desk. "Offenders often devise twisted versions of the truth. In the cases you mentioned, their mission is to attain the happily-ever-after ending of fairy tales for their victims. Again, because they believe they are saviors of sorts, they use that excuse to commit murder. Their objective is 'to save' their victims, so to speak, regardless of the pain they inflict."

"You mentioned that the burnt matches symbolize hope to the killer. Could they symbolize anything else?"

"They could represent a symbolic burning to the killer. He believes his victims need to suffer as part of the human experience to find the meaning of life."

"To find the meaning of life?" I echoed. "How ridiculous!"

A tiny smile played on her lips. "It sounds ludicrous, but it's his way of thinking. Senseless things happen in our sane world that we're unable to comprehend sometimes."

I'd heard enough to support the killer's motives in our three cases. I thanked Laura and drove to the unit. What awaited me there was a revelation I hadn't anticipated.

Forensics delivered the results from the lab tests performed on Bill Hardy's magazine that Ryan and I had recovered from a trash bin in a park. They reported an inconclusive comparison of the fingerprints on the magazine to those on the burnt matches found near Susan Kendall's body. Similarly, a comparison of his fingerprints to those on the matches left with the other two female victims proved inconclusive.

The report explained that the fingerprints in all three cases couldn't be identified due to an insufficient quantity or clarity of skin features on the evidence. Consequently, it was impossible to determine that they came from the same source.

I reacted to the news. "This report doesn't eliminate any of our three potential suspects. Right, Ryan?"

"Right," he said. "Unfortunately, it doesn't mean they're guilty either."

Matt added his interpretation. "Partial fingerprints on the matches. I'd say the perp took extra care to prevent making the same mistake at subsequent crime scenes."

"Which could include many more we've yet to discover," Ryan said, his tone cynical.

I scanned the forensic report. "What about the DNA test on the cigarette butt that Bill ditched?" I asked Ryan.

"It's going to take the lab more time to process, if at all," he said. "It was badly damaged."

I steered the conversation in another direction and adopted Laura's analysis. "If we study these cases in relation to the fairy-tale premise, the killer is showing his power over innocent victims by leaving the matches. It's his way of willing them to burn and suffer, whatever his reason."

Ryan agreed. "It's a fair analysis. The anonymous caller indicated as much with that quote about burning. It ties in with what I said before. The perp attains his goals and leaves the matches behind as his signature."

"Some signature," Matt muttered. "The guy leaves us his calling card, and we can't even find him."

I understood Matt's frustration. With Christmas days away, the prospect that we'd solve at least one of the cold cases was diminishing. We were undeniably closing in on the killer, but who was he and where was he?

"Matt, don't you have a meeting scheduled with that new witness who called you?" Ryan asked him.

"Yep, early tomorrow morning with Carl Armstrong," Matt said with a renewed surge of enthusiasm. "He told me he dated Michelle Roy and Pamela Cooper. I can't wait to interview him."

Optimism had resurfaced, along with a revival of hope. A tiny piece of evidence might materialize from Matt's meeting and help us solve these cases. It had happened before. All we needed was a bit of good luck.

I mentally squared my shoulders and held my chin up. Yes, I had to believe.

32

———

Matt arrived at the unit the next morning after his meeting with a man who claimed to have dated two of our female victims days before they were murdered. "Hey, guys! Wait till you hear this!" He placed an evidence bag on his desk, then sat in his chair facing Ryan and me.

Judging from the excitement bubbling inside him, it had to be good news. Possibly even the break we were waiting for.

"My interview with Carl Armstrong went well," Matt said. "He told me he used to visit a pub in Cedarberry in his younger days. That's where he met Michelle Roy and Pamela Cooper on separate occasions. He dated one, then the other. Before the relationship got serious with either of the women, they disappeared. Then he learned about their deaths. One after the other."

"What's in the evidence bag, Matt?" Ryan asked.

"I'm getting to that," Matt said with a playful grin. "Anyway, Carl happens to be a collector. You'll never guess what he collects?"

"It had better be something useful to our investigation," Ryan said.

"Matchbooks." Matt picked up the evidence bag. "This is a matchbook from the pub where he met the two women decades ago."

I studied the tiny square form. Printed in shiny letters on a black background was the name, The Silver Anchor. "You think there's a connection to the matches left with our three victims?"

"That's what I'm hoping for," Matt said, beaming. "It means our perp visited the same pub as the two women."

"Let's get your sample to forensics and ask them if they can compare the matches inside it to the burnt matches in our three cases," Ryan said. "By the way, Carl had told you he might be able to describe the guy. Did he?"

"He said he was slim but muscular, and kind of gentle with the women," Matt said. "He seemed to compete with other guys for dates. Carl told me he was really upset when he thought the guy stole his girlfriends from him."

I was curious. "Why did he think he stole them?"

"Carl hadn't had the chance to advance his relationship with Michelle or Pamela. He'd dated each woman only once. One night around the Christmas holidays, he saw the guy leave the pub with Michelle. The next week it was with Pamela. Carl was a regular at the pub. He said he didn't see either woman there again. Or the mystery guy. After he discovered the women had been murdered, he had his suspicions. He didn't have the courage to come forward until now."

"Why now?" I asked.

"One of his old drinking buddies recognized the two women on our police website and told Carl about it," Matt said. "He persuaded Carl to follow up and call the police."

"Could Carl identify the man he saw in the pub?" Ryan asked him.

"Only from memory," Matt said. "If he had to identify him from a photo or a police lineup, forget it. Carl lost his eyesight years ago."

The unit received a surprise visitor later in the day. After Debra Robinson had been cleared by security and escorted into the conference room, Ryan and I sat down with her.

"I wanted to give you this in person." Debra slid a rectangular box across the table to me. "I've held onto it long enough. It's Susan's diary."

I held back from touching the box for reasons known to Ryan and me. "This is totally unexpected. Thank you, Debra."

Ryan reached for the box and opened it. Inside was a faded pink diary with a lock. A tiny key hung from a latch that bound the diary. "How did you get this, Debra?"

"Susan forgot it at my place the night she left. I haven't unlocked it or read it since."

"Why bring it to us now?" I asked her.

"Long story." Debra sighed. "I've been following your police website, the one that features the cold cases of young women who have been murdered. I felt guilty for not telling you about Susan's diary the last time I saw you, but I wanted to respect her private thoughts. With the reopening of her case, I decided it was time to hand it over. There might something useful to your investigations in it."

"We appreciate you coming to us with this," Ryan said to her.

"There's another reason I brought you the diary," Debra said. "I'm hoping the information in there is of value to you and will prevent you from charging the wrong person for Suzie's murder."

The day was full of surprises. "What do you mean?" I asked her.

"You might have a certain suspect in mind. I'm asking you not to rely on rumors to solve Susan's case. That's all." She stood up, a sign that she refused to say anything more.

Ryan thanked her again and escorted her out.

I reflected on what Debra meant about relying on rumors. She'd believed the rumors about Richard Kendall's abusive nature toward his family, hadn't she? And what about Kenneth Cameron's rich family disowning him if he married a "poor" girl? Didn't she accept that rumor as the truth too?

Was she trying to purposely lead us to the killer? Or away from him?

33

———

After Ryan returned to the conference room, we remained there to read Susan's diary. It might give us important details about her killer, and we couldn't wait to unlock it. That Debra Robinson had dropped it off was not only timely but also raised our hopes.

Ryan handed it to me. "Here, Amber. Do your thing."

As soon as I touched the pink diary, a panorama of faces swept through my mind. I placed the diary on the table. "We'll have to take it slowly. There's a lot in here."

Ryan picked up the diary. "How about I unlock it? We can examine it together. Then we'll brief Matt about what we found."

I watched as he used the tiny key to unlock it. We were about to pry into the intimate thoughts of a young woman who believed that a hopeful future was within her grasp.

Ryan flipped through the pages. "Susan must have bought this diary halfway through the year. From January right through the early summer months, there are no notations."

"She started her job at the diner in the summer. Maybe she didn't have time to write every day."

"The first entry is on August 23." He read the passage out loud:

"Debra has been so generous for letting me sleep on her couch the past month, even though I can barely afford the small monthly rent I owe her. I eat twice a day and cut back on other stuff to save money. Bill refused to give me a raise again. Lucky for me, the tips are good. When I agreed to our hookup last week, he promised he'd give me a raise. He didn't. I'll ask him again soon."

"A hookup?" I said, astounded. "Susan slept with Bill so she could get a raise?"

Ryan shook his head in disgust. "What a lowlife that guy is." He flipped through more pages. "There's nothing more until this September 1 entry."

"I asked Bill for a raise again. He said no. I won't give up. I can't. This is the only job I can get in this town."

Her words burst with desperation. "I can't imagine working for someone like that. What a struggle Susan had!"

Ryan turned more pages. "The next entry is on September 15."

"I met an amazing guy name Ken. Handsome and smart. He wants to be a doctor. We've only been dating a couple of weeks, but I'm in love! I'm sure the feeling is mutual. Last night, we had a romantic dinner at a fancy restaurant in another town. I told Debra not to wait up for me."

"This fact gives us the timeline in her relationship with Ken," I said.

"It explains why he believed the baby was his," Ryan said.

I ventured another guess. "It could be Bill's baby!"

"That's to be determined," he cautioned me. "Susan wrote more on October 20."

"I've been feeling sick lately. It's because I don't eat very well. Bill said no to a raise again. I'm through asking him. I should have known he was never going to give it to me like he promised, the scrooge. Why did I think I was different from the other girls he slept with. I'm not surprised they quit!"

"Debra had told us about the turnover in staff," I said. "Susan's diary now confirms what caused it."

Ryan flipped through the pages. "The next entry is on November 15."

"Devon asked me out on a date again. I lost count of how many times. I already told him I had a steady boyfriend, but he doesn't get the message. He's sweet, but I'm just not attracted to him. I feel sorry for him, especially after the terrible way that Bill treats him. I hope he finds a girlfriend soon."

"The next notation is on November 29," Ryan said.

"The doc confirmed I was almost three months pregnant. I told Bill. I asked him for extra money for the baby. He refused. We got into a fight about it. He said it wasn't his problem. He threatened me about telling anyone. If word got out that it was his baby, he said I'd regret it. He scares me!"

I took in a quick breath. "It was Bill's baby! I was right. What if she never told Kenneth she was pregnant with another man's child?"

"We can't jump to conclusions," Ryan said. "What if Susan had relations with other men? Lisa said she had dated others."

"They can't be important. Susan didn't mention them in her diary." Then I remembered. "Oh...there was Ernie, her prom date, who called the Info-Crime line. He said they were 'pretty close,' but he stopped dating her by July. So August, September, October, November...that's four months by my count. Susan wrote that she was almost three months' pregnant. Ernie wasn't the father."

"Let's read on," Ryan said. "Susan's next entry is on December 6."

"I can't tell Ken I'm pregnant. He'd never believe it was his. We were careful. Well, most of the time. Anyways, if he knew I was pregnant, it would ruin his plans for medical school. He might even refuse to marry me! No, I'll keep it to myself for now."

"The next entry is on December 14."

"I don't want my relationship with Ken to be based on lies. I decided to tell him I was pregnant. I showed him the ultrasound photo of the baby. He was thrilled! We made plans to leave Willowburg soon and get married in another town."

Sadness welled inside me as I considered the likelihood that I'd been wrong about Kenneth. For one reason or another, he could have killed Susan.

Ryan flipped through the rest of the diary. "There's one last entry on December 24."

"It's Christmas Eve! I'm quitting my job at five o'clock today. Yay! Let's see how Bill handles the busy restaurant till ten tonight without me. Ken is meeting me after work in front of the flower shop, and we're leaving town. I can't wait to start our new life together!"

I felt sick to my stomach.

34

The next day's revelation added one more key element to Susan Kendall's case file. The result from a forensic test revealed that Bill Hardy had indeed fathered her baby.

"Bill just made the leap to the top of the list as a prime suspect," Matt said. "It confirms what you told me Susan wrote in her diary, Ryan. Way to go!"

Ryan pursed his lips. "I'm not so sure."

"About what?"

"I have my doubts about Bill. His motive wasn't that strong."

"Not strong?" Matt rolled his eyes in disbelief. "Bill withheld information from us. He didn't tell us he slept with Susan or knew about her pregnancy."

"Neither did Kenneth," I said. "What's worse, Kenneth's fingerprints were on the ultrasound photo. He lied about Susan having shown it to him."

"Don't get me wrong," Ryan said. "Whatever their motives were, these men remain potential suspects. Proving which one killed those women is the challenge we continue to face."

"How about visiting Bill Hardy to test his reaction to the news?" I asked Ryan.

"Excellent idea," he said. "This time, I'll go with you. Matt, we need to narrow the timeline for these potential perps. Try to find an event, a date, or something else that undeniably ties them to Susan's murder."

"And to the other two murders," Matt added. "It means digging for more facts."

"Exactly." Ryan turned to me. "Let's pay Bill Hardy another surprise visit."

Bill opened the door to his apartment but kept it slightly ajar. "Not you guys again. What is it this time?"

"There's been a development," Ryan said. "May we come in?"

Bill let us in and stood by the door after he closed it. Like the last time, he didn't invite us into the living room, so we remained standing in the hallway.

The first question out of Ryan's mouth was, "Bill, did you ever have an intimate relationship with Susan Kendall?"

Bill's jaw tightened but he remained calm. "Yes. We were both consenting adults. She didn't report me to the police, did she?" he scoffed, as if it were a joke.

"You tell me." Ryan's tone was firm. "Should she have reported you?"

Bill's expression froze. He recovered in the next moment. "Believe me, it was a one-time fling. Nobody got hurt."

I questioned his comment. "Nobody got hurt. What's that supposed to mean?"

"I didn't force her to sleep with me," Bill said with an air of arrogance.

I set up the question that would lead to the big reveal. "Do you remember how we told you Susan was pregnant when she was killed?"

"Yes," he said. "So what? I wasn't responsible for keeping track of my staff's social life."

I delighted in giving him the news. "A forensic test confirms you were the father of Susan's unborn child."

Bill didn't flinch. "You're kidding."

"No," I said. "It was your baby."

Ryan jumped in. "Did Susan ever request financial support from you for her unborn child?"

Bill's gaze fell to the floor. "Like I told you the last time you were here, I didn't even know she was pregnant."

He was lying.

Ryan used the details in Susan's diary to support his next claim. "We have a witness statement that confirms you and Susan were arguing about money the day she quit her job. She told you about the pregnancy and asked you for child support."

"Look, we've been through this idiotic business before." Bill raised his arms in annoyance and let them fall to his side with a thump. "My talk with Susan was about her asking me for a raise. Period."

"Why would she ask you for a raise when she was planning to quit her job and leave town that very same day?" I asked him.

Bill's eyes darkened as he spit out the words. "It was about a raise. That's all it was, dammit."

He'd stated the facts to his benefit. Our conversation was going nowhere.

Ryan put an end to it. "Thanks for your time, Bill. We haven't completed our investigation. We might have more questions for you in the future."

"Suit yourself." Bill jerked open the door to let us out, then bolted it shut behind us.

As we buckled up in the car, I said to Ryan, "What a heartless man! He didn't even show an ounce of interest in the fact he'd fathered Susan's baby."

"Certain people are born with no conscience," he said,

steering the car onto the main street. "Or at the least, no empathy."

No empathy. No ethics. No remorse. It summed up the challenge we were facing in finding a cold-blooded murderer.

35

––––––––

The weekend flew by with grocery shopping, home chores, and catching up on sleep filling the time. Even Nicole called to say she couldn't get together. She had class rehearsals for the Christmas play that the school was presenting to parents this week.

Monday arrived soon enough, and with it, a lingering mood of uncertainty. It was one thing to accept that we'd reached an impasse in our investigations. It was quite another to explain the situation to Lieutenant Payton. Lucky for us, the lieutenant was occupied with phone calls and meetings and didn't ask us for an update.

Ryan gathered Matt and me in the conference room. "We're at a standstill," he said, his manner gloomy. "We need to revisit the facts to see if we overlooked something."

"But Ryan," Matt whined, "what more can we do? We've interviewed everyone, a few of them at least twice. Did it get us any further? No."

"Then we need to determine where we went wrong," Ryan persisted. "Did we ask the right questions? Did we probe further into—" An incoming call was transferred to him. After a brief conversation, he relayed the news to us. "The long-term care home called me. Richard Kendall passed away this morning."

"Now we're down to two," Matt said.

Ryan raised a hand. "Hold on. Not so fast. Richard's death doesn't eliminate him from our investigation."

"Why not?"

"Because witnesses have told us that the guy had a violent background. He was an alcoholic and known to police for unruly behavior in bars. Witnesses have confirmed he beat his wife and daughter, even though no charges were laid. Besides, we haven't cleared him yet. Unless we can prove someone else murdered Susan Kendall and the other two women, Richard Kendall stays on our list."

Matt turned to me for support. "What do you think, Amber?"

I refused to take part in their tug-of-war argument. "All three suspects are potentially guilty. I'm not sure about any of them anymore."

"Don't give up, Amber," Ryan pleaded. "There must be something over the top about one of these guys that stands out to you."

He was right. Something was nagging at me about one of them. "Okay. I admit I now have doubts about Kenneth Cameron's innocence. Mainly because he lied to us about the ultrasound photo. His fingerprints were all over it. He had the ultimate motive to get rid of Susan: the success of his future and prosperous career as a doctor."

"Oh...and let's not forget the scandal a pregnant girlfriend would have created for his rich family," Matt said, waggling his eyebrows. "Especially if they discovered later that it wasn't his baby."

"We've already considered the alternate scenario," I said, gathering momentum. "If Kenneth saw the ultrasound photo and believed it wasn't his baby, did he kill Susan out of a sense of betrayal? Did the comfort of money inspire confidence that he could get away with murder?"

Ryan concurred. "It has potential as a motive."

"If we're rehashing stuff, I'll give it a try," Matt said. "What if Bill and Susan were arguing about child support the day she died? It means she knew it was his baby. Maybe he knew it too. Bill had a reputation for threatening his employees if they didn't do what he wanted. His staff feared him. Imagine if the popular owner of your local diner bribes one of his female employees to sleep with him, gets her pregnant, and the whole town finds out about it? What an embarrassment! It would ruin his reputation as the best employer around. If you ask me, that's a pretty strong motive for murder."

"It could well be," Ryan said.

Our conversation energized me. "One more thing," I said. "All three men traveled back then. They had easy access to towns bordering Willowburg."

"Speaking of travel..." Ryan said. "Matt, did you find anything that could narrow the timeline and location of the murders for any of these guys?"

"I reviewed every bit of file data," Matt said. "I found no specific event or date that pinpoints that criteria to any of them. Sorry, Ryan."

Worry lines crossed Ryan's forehead but he continued. "Okay. We have reasonably strong arguments against our three potential suspects. I'll say it again. What we need is more evidence. Solid evidence. If we had it, we could prove that one of these guys lied to us about his alibi."

At Ryan's mention of an alibi, something else came to light. "What about Richard Kendall's alibi? Lisa said she wasn't sure he was home that evening before Kenneth arrived."

I'd have laughed at the dumbfounded expressions on the men's faces if the question hadn't been so serious.

"You're absolutely right," Matt said. "But we can't ask him. He's dead."

"I can ask Lisa," I said. "I can try to jog her memory."

"Give her a call," Ryan said to me. "Tell her we're on speakerphone."

I reached Lisa on her day off. She was astonished to hear from me but agreed to answer my question about her father.

"Like I told you," Lisa said, "he drank that night and fell asleep in front of the fireplace. I had to add logs to keep the fireplace going."

"Logs? You didn't mention that before."

She inhaled a gulp of air. "Oh, I just remembered. After he overheard my phone conversation with Susan and ranted about her pregnancy and the shame of it all, he went outside to chop wood. Then he brought some logs inside."

"How long was he outdoors?"

"Oh...at least an hour."

"Are you sure he was chopping wood the whole time?"

"I think so, but..." Lisa hesitated. "I mean, I was on the phone with my friends. He could have been outdoors longer."

I pressed on. "Then what happened?"

"When he came back inside, he was angry with me because dinner was cold. He ate it anyway. Then he went to the living room and started to drink. He fell asleep there."

"What time did you add logs to the fireplace?"

"Um...it was around nine o'clock."

"And your father was still asleep in the living room?" I asked.

"Yes, until Kenneth arrived at about ten," Lisa said. "At least, I think he was there all that time."

It was all I needed to hear. I thanked Lisa and ended the call.

"And then there were two," Matt repeated.

"If you want to give a dead man the benefit of the doubt," Ryan said.

Matt gaped at him. "Don't you believe Lisa? She said her father was home."

"Lisa put a doubt in my mind," Ryan said. "Richard could have easily driven to town and back within the hour that she thought he was outside chopping wood. She was on the phone and wouldn't have noticed if he was gone fifteen minutes or longer. She couldn't even confirm if he was asleep in the living room during the hour before Kenneth arrived." He looked at me. "That was a good call, Amber."

"Thanks," I said.

Ryan went on. "Similarly, Kenneth Cameron and Bill Hardy told us where they were the evening Susan was murdered. The major setback is that we haven't been able to confirm their alibis to the extent we could clear them."

"How can we?" Matt exclaimed. "It's next to impossible. You're talking decades ago."

Ryan repeated his usual refrain. "That's why I keep saying we need solid evidence."

Back to square one.

36

Lieutenant Payton gathered the team in his office for an informal meeting the next morning. Informal or not, with everything else that had happened lately, I dreaded the worst.

The lieutenant remained standing. "I've received calls from local police investigators wanting to discuss an article that recently appeared in a city newspaper. It cited the job requirements for investigative officers. Of special note were 'gut instincts' that can help them find perpetrators when physical evidence is lacking." The lieutenant surveyed us as a group and didn't single anyone out.

"Sir, why were they calling *you* about the article?" Ryan asked.

"I'm assuming they linked it to the gossip that's been circulating about Amber and her unique abilities," the lieutenant said matter-of-factly, then reverted to his original topic. "Although the source of this article wasn't confirmed, I thought it prudent to share the piece with all investigative units in town. Consequently, I did. I suggested that it be presented as a reminder to our colleagues regarding the little voice that warns them about imminent threats or dangerous felons. It's an attribute that the more skilled officers recognize as a 'gut feeling' because they've used it instinctively and frequently in the line of duty."

"Sir, do you believe it'll help quash the rumors about Amber?" Matt asked him.

"I trust it already has. The calls have stopped." He smiled briefly. "I pinned a copy to the community board in the kitchen for all of you to read. I won't keep you any longer. Get on with your work."

I stopped by the kitchen to read the article that the lieutenant had pinned on the corkboard. The writer was listed as unknown. As I touched the newspaper clipping, I perceived an image of the lieutenant tapping on the keyboard at his desk. On his computer screen were lines from the newspaper article.

I hid my amusement. Lieutenant Payton's strategy had worked. Writing and anonymously publishing the article, then distributing copies of it to police investigators must have added chuckles to his day.

It would be our little secret.

Forensics returned with their analysis of the matchbook that Carl Armstrong had offered us from his vintage collection. The results were conclusive: The matches were the same as the ones found at the crime scene for each of the three female victims.

"That's wild!" Matt almost sprang from his chair. "It proves without a doubt that we're looking for the same perp."

I shared his enthusiasm. "It also means he was a regular at The Silver Anchor. We're getting closer."

"It's what we're hoping for," Ryan said as he leaned against my desk. "Now, I don't want to stifle your enthusiasm—"

"Uh-oh," I said. "There's a 'but' coming."

"Sort of." Ryan shrugged. "The fact that the perp killed

these women and dropped their bodies in three different locations doesn't help us to find him. We need more evidence."

Our discussion was interrupted when Nadia transferred a call from the Info-Crime line to my desk. "This one's a real number," she said to me, her tone sarcastic. "And I don't mean mathematical. It's a recording."

I took the call. While I waited for the caller to speak, music floated to my ears. I recognized the famous song right away. It was "Michelle" by The Beatles.

Was this someone's idea of a sick joke?

The song played for a few more seconds, then a metallic, disguised voice came on. "You're messing with the wrong person. It's not going to end well for you if you don't stop trying to find me."

A hazy image of a man charging at me with a large knife flashed across my mind. The same man as in earlier calls! I shuddered but held my ground.

The caller said, "This is your final warning." The line went dead.

Nadia was right. The threatening call had been prerecorded. What's more, the caller sounded desperate. It was a sign we were narrowing the gap to finding him. I shared my perceptions with Ryan and Matt.

After they listened to the recorded call, Matt said, "No sane person who saw the website page on Michelle Roy would pull a stunt like that. The song the caller chose tells me he's a lunatic. It must be our perp."

"You know what they say," Ryan said. "Dead people don't call the Info-Crime line."

"Which leaves Richard Kendall permanently off our list," Matt said. "Now we're officially down to two."

Torn between choosing which one of our two suspects was the real killer, I trusted the insights I'd perceived up to now. But who was the angry man wielding a large knife that my brain had captured in brief snapshots?

Was it Kenneth Cameron, the calm-and-collected doctor who claimed he didn't know Susan Kendall was pregnant, let alone with another man's baby? Was it Bill Hardy, the overbearing, short-tempered owner of a diner who was overheard arguing with Susan Kendall supposedly about child support minutes before she quit her job? Or was it someone else who had eluded our suspicions altogether?

While Matt and Ryan worked at their desks, I reflected on the evidence in our three cases, the likely motives behind the killing of the women, the witness statements against our potential suspects, the forensics reports supporting our suspicions...

The anonymous caller on the Info-Crime line had warned us to stop investigating. Why? Were we getting close? Or did he believe we were following the wrong leads? If so, did he want to make sure he got the credit for the crimes and not someone else?

Frustration ran through my veins. We'd done everything right and followed the logic. And yet, we'd failed to solve the cases we were working on. Why?

There could only be one answer. Someone along the way had lied to us. Someone whose witness statement we'd believed to be truthful had deceived us. Someone who had skewed our suspicions, narrowed our train of thought, and taken our investigation offtrack.

As the pieces of the puzzle began to fit, the identity of the real killer became clearer to me. Like Ryan had often repeated, all I needed was physical proof. How on earth would I dig that up from the 1980s?

37

Holding a rectangular parcel in gloved hands, Corey hurried over to my desk after lunch. "This special delivery has been cleared. It's addressed to the unit. Which one of you wants to open it?" His eyes darted from me to Ryan to Matt.

Ryan rose from his chair. "I'll take it."

Corey waited while Ryan put on a pair of vinyl gloves. After he handed Ryan the parcel, he dashed back to his desk.

Ryan examined the brown paper wrapping on the box. "It doesn't have a return address. Don't we love surprises?"

"This I have to see." Matt got up from his chair and approached to get a better look.

I remained seated. The only surprise I wanted was evidence to confirm that my suspicions about the killer were correct.

Ryan removed the paper wrapping and the lid. Inside the box was an item covered in layers of plastic wrap, followed by butcher paper. His jaw dropped as he unwrapped the final sheet and held up the item. "It's a large kitchen knife. And it has dried blood on it!"

I jumped to my feet and rushed over to Ryan, my pulse racing. "It can't be the murder weapon. Can it?"

Matt joined us. "It could be the sicko playing a joke on us again."

Ryan peered inside the box. "There's a note in here." He picked it up and read it:

"Sorry I lied to you, but I was scared as hell as long as Bill Hardy was alive. My doc told me I have cancer and only six months to live. I wanted to do something good before I died. I'm sending you an eight-inch chef's knife. I found it in the garbage behind Bill's diner on Christmas Eve when Susan died. I wrapped it as best I could and kept it in my freezer all these years."

The note was signed *Devon Hill*.

I was speechless.

Matt blabbered for both of us. "Do you get what this means? It's the murder weapon. This is unbelievable! Now we can arrest Bill Hardy for murder. And Devon Hill for withholding evidence."

"Not so fast," Ryan said. "We need proof that the knife is a valid piece of evidence. If it is and Devon kept it in a freezer, the blood might not be contaminated. We'll send it to forensics to include DNA and fingerprint testing. We'll put a rush on it, then take it from there."

"Yes...yes, of course," Matt stammered with excitement. "That's what I meant."

Ryan placed the knife back in the box but stopped from wrapping it. "Amber, do you want to—"

"I'll give it a try." I pulled out a pair of vinyl gloves from the pack on his desk and slipped them on. I gently touched the blade of the knife with one finger.

A woman's screams weakened my legs and jolted me off balance. I leaned forward on Ryan's desk for support.

Ryan took hold of my arms to steady me. "Are you okay?"

"Yes," I said, straightening up. "I'm not done. I need to continue."

"Are you sure?"

"Yes." I touched the handle this time. I captured the image of an angry man plunging the knife once, twice... He sustained his ruthless attack, but I stayed strong, struggling to distinguish the features of his face in the blurry image. Gasping for air, I broke away and gripped the amethyst crystal in my pocket. "Sorry. I tried. I can't see the killer's face."

"It's okay." Ryan's voice was calm. "We can imagine the nightmare you experience every time you handle evidence."

"Let me tell you what I saw." I described the irate man and his repulsive rage.

Impressed by my portrayal of the caller, Matt let out a low whistle. "Like I said, we're hunting for a lunatic." He scratched his head. "Another thing. If Kenneth was our mystery caller, he wouldn't have used the song 'Michelle' in his recording. He was dating Susan. There are lots of songs with Susan or Sue in them. By elimination, Bill Hardy is our most likely suspect."

"We'll have to play out this round first before we jump to conclusions." Ryan carefully rewrapped the knife in the butcher paper and plastic wrap and placed it back into the box. "Whoever our perp is, he killed Susan, then he killed Michelle and Pamela weeks later. He's alive today and celebrating each of their deaths, in whatever order, with their names in songs."

"Point taken," Matt said. "I don't understand why my focus was only on Susan's case." He looked away, annoyed by his blunder.

"One of our witnesses lied to us," I blurted, producing more flabbergasted stares from my two colleagues.

"How do you know that?" Matt asked.

"In the lieutenant's words, call it a gut feeling," I said. "My instincts tell me Devon lied about Bill leaving the diner to go get supplies. Debra said she didn't see Bill leave."

"Debra told us the place was busy," Ryan said. "Maybe she didn't see him leave."

I stood by my argument. "Maybe she didn't see Devon leave either."

"What are you getting at?" Ryan asked me.

It was time to reveal my suspicions. "What if the killer wasn't Bill Hardy? What if it wasn't Kenneth Cameron either? Call me cynical, but after all the work we've done, we're getting nowhere. I have the feeling we've overlooked a suspect."

"Who?"

"Devon Hill."

Matt gawked at me "Are you kidding?"

"Matt, don't you remember Bill telling us he sent Devon out to buy supplies around dinnertime because they were running short?"

His expression lit up. "Oh, hell! I completely forgot about that."

"There's more," I said. "Susan wrote in her diary how Devon often asked her to go out with him. She refused every time. The rejections could have made him feel inferior and frustrated."

"So, he snapped," Matt added.

"It's possible," Ryan said.

I wasn't finished defending my argument. "It's quite the coincidence that Devon found a second body in a different town. And now he sends us a knife that's guaranteed to have his fingerprints on it because he handled it. Bill's fingerprints are certainly on it if he used it at the diner."

Awareness glowed in Ryan's eyes. "Amber, you might be onto something important. I'll send forensics the knife and the note Devon included with it. If we're lucky, they'll be able to match the partial prints on the matches found at the crime scenes to Devon's fingerprints on these items."

"Right on!" Matt pumped a fist in the air. "There's no telling how many cold cases we'll solve now."

"We can eliminate Kenneth Cameron and Richard

Kendall," I said. "Unless forensics finds their fingerprints or DNA on the knife."

"That would really mess things up for us." Ryan brought us back to reality. "I don't want to raise anyone's hopes just yet. If forensics can't test the knife in time, we'll need to come up with a strategy to catch our perp, whoever he is."

"We should interview Devon again," Matt said. "Put the pressure on him."

"On the contrary," Ryan said. "We need to approach him as an ally. We absolutely need his cooperation. We can arrange for Devon and Bill to meet."

"You mean, like a showdown?" Matt asked.

"Something like that," Ryan said. "More like a face-to-face meeting between them. It'll ensure more authentic reactions. Neither of them will know that we'll be operating a sting operation around their little get-together to catch the real perp."

"Will Devon agree to help us is the question," I said. "He might not want to see Bill again."

"He doesn't have a choice," Ryan said. "He sent us the knife and hopes we'll arrest Bill."

I had another question for him. "How will you sell Devon on our plan?"

"I'll make the offer more interesting by telling him there's a reward for Bill's capture. If we get his support, we'll put our plan in motion."

"If Devon thinks the cops are on his side," Matt said, "he'll be thrilled to assist us."

Something told me it wasn't going to be that easy.

38

Days later, forensics confirmed that the blood on the eight-inch kitchen knife was indeed a match for Susan Kendall's blood. They also confirmed that the fingerprints on the knife belonged to Devon Hill and Bill Hardy.

"That's not surprising," Ryan said after he'd read out the report to Matt and me. "Either of them could have used that knife at the diner."

"If Devon used it to kill Susan," I said, "he'd make sure he didn't wipe Bill's prints off the handle so he could claim Bill committed the crime."

"That was pretty smart of him," Matt said.

"There's more." Ryan scanned the report. "Forensics couldn't match the fingerprints from Bill or Devon to the partial prints on the matches found at the three crime scenes."

"We have the knife," Matt said. "It's a vital piece of evidence. Right?"

"If we can make use of it to expose the real perp," Ryan said.

"Whoever that turns out to be," said Matt, wryly.

Ryan moved on. "Okay. Let's put our heads together and come up with a foolproof strategy to catch this guy."

We brainstormed different scenarios and agreed on a feasible plan we'd put into action within the next twenty-four hours. The grim reality was that a clear-cut solution to our three cases depended on Devon Hill. His agreement to play along with us would determine the success or failure of our strategy.

While Ryan talked to Devon on speakerphone in the conference room, Matt and I sat by and listened in. Devon was our last and only chance to solve our three cases.

Ryan thanked him for sending us a valuable piece of evidence. His tone grew firm when he explained the plan we wanted him to take part in. "Devon, your cooperation would help the police immensely."

"Well, I-I..." Devon stuttered. "I'm afraid to —"

"Don't you want to help us put this guy behind bars?"

"I-I don't know."

"There might even be a reward for Bill's capture."

"A reward? How much?"

"Fifty thousand dollars."

The suspense was overwhelming. Devon had to say yes, or it would be a major setback for us.

Devon's brittle voice filled the room. "Let me get this straight. You want me to call Bill and tell him I have proof he killed Susan? If he wants the knife back, he has to pay me up front."

"Tell him you're going to tell the cops about the knife if he doesn't give you the money," Ryan said.

A long moment of silence filled the air. Had Devon ended the call?

Ryan spoke. "Devon? Are you there?"

There was a rustling sound on the other end of the line as Devon adjusted his phone. "Where am I supposed to meet Bill?"

"Outside the city core. We'll choose the location. You just

need to show up. I can drive you over there, but Bill might spot the unmarked car. Can you get a lift there instead?"

More hesitation. "I got a friend who lends me his car sometimes."

"I have to warn you. It might be a dangerous situation."

"Ha! Not more dangerous than what I'm facing now."

"Is that a yes, Devon? Are you going to help us put this guy in jail?"

We held our collective breaths. I crossed my fingers that Devon would accept to meet with Bill as part of our sting operation. If he refused, we'd have to come up with a different strategy.

"Okay," Devon said. "What have I got to lose? I'm almost dead anyway. Fifty thousand can buy me a nice trip around the world."

"I'll get in touch with you when things are set up." Ryan ended the call.

"Way to go, Ryan!" Matt gave him a thumbs-up.

"That was the easy part," Ryan said with relief. "We'll get a warrant for the operation and set up police surveillance in an abandoned commercial building. Outside the city core is preferable and safer if anything unforeseen happens."

"What about the knife Devon sent us?" I asked. "We can't use that."

"We have a contact that can make a clone identical to the real thing, blood markings and all, within twenty-four hours," Ryan said.

"What's next?" Matt asked him.

"After everything is set up, I'll go visit Devon while he calls Bill. He'll threaten Bill with going to the police unless he pays him the money. If Bill agrees to the meeting, he'll give him the time and location. The success of our secret maneuver depends on how convincing Devon will be and how Bill reacts. One slip-up and it could be fatal for either of them—and our operation."

I inserted a limitation to Ryan's rationale. "What if Bill is innocent? He might brush off Devon's threat and refuse to meet with him altogether."

Ryan shrugged. "That's a risk we'll have to take. If Bill accepts his invitation, it means he has something to hide."

"Is there anything else we can do, Ryan?" Matt asked. "I mean, as a backup."

"Yes. I'll request a search warrant for both their apartments while they're away. It could turn up additional evidence."

Based on my insights, I was certain who the real killer was. How Devon Hill had flown under the radar all this time was baffling. Ironically, the success of our sting operation depended entirely on him now.

Ryan listened in as Devon made the call to Bill on speaker-phone. After Devon convinced Bill that he had a dark secret that would put him in jail for the rest of his life, Bill agreed to meet with him.

How successfully the police sting would unfold was anyone's guess.

39

———

The abandoned factory on the south shore of Montreal would have provided the perfect setting for a thriller movie this evening. Except this was no movie. It was a meeting between Devon Hill and Bill Hardy. One way or another, the next minutes would reveal which one of these men was the real killer.

Police surveillance of the area surrounding the factory was heavy, with forces covering the main and side streets leading to the building. Capturing a serial killer was no small feat. He'd escaped law enforcement for decades and was an expert in getting away with the alleged murder of three women.

As planned, Devon drove up in an old-model white car an hour before his meeting time. The sun had already set, but a quick pass of Ryan's flashlight revealed dents and scrapes in the neglected vehicle. Devon parked the car close to the front entrance so Bill would see it when he arrived.

After Ryan made sure Devon was in position inside the building, he joined me in an unmarked car safely hidden behind a huge container. From our location, one of the side doors to the building was visible. We would view the developing scene inside the factory by way of a laptop connected to the surveillance system that Corey and the tech team had set up.

Minutes before Bill's scheduled arrival time, we received word from the surveillance team that he had driven up in a dark car. From the view on our laptop, we saw Bill entering the front door to the dimly lit building. He crossed the floor toward Devon and stopped, keeping several feet between them.

"You got a hell of a nerve threatening me to show up here," Bill said. "I had to pay for a car rental on top of it."

"My heart bleeds for you," Devon snickered. "You bring the money?"

Bill raised his voice. "Is that all you have to say to me after all these years?"

"You killed Susan Kendall. I have proof."

"What kind of proof?"

Devon kicked a dark garbage bag at his feet. The movement threw him off-balance, but he straightened up quickly. "Physical proof."

Bill gestured toward Devon. "Look at you. You're nothing but a stoned old man. A junkie. You think the cops would believe you?"

"They will when I show them this." Devon removed the knife from the garbage bag and held it up.

Bill gaped at him. "Where did you get that?"

"You threw it out in the garbage behind the diner after you killed Susan. I went back that night to get it."

"You're lying."

"Nope. Your fingerprints are on the knife."

"It doesn't mean anything," Bill said. "I used knives like that every day to prepare meals at the diner."

"Yeah, but this one has your prints *and* Susan's blood on it." Devon waved the knife in the air. "The day that she quit her job, I heard her tell you she was carrying your baby. Yes, Bill, *your* baby."

Ryan and I exchanged astonished looks. Devon knew Susan was pregnant!

"Then you gave me the lousy excuse that we needed kitchen supplies," Devon smirked. "You lied! What you did was run out after Susan to keep her quiet for good. You killed her!"

These two men were so convincing that I was starting to doubt myself. Had I been wrong in believing that Devon was the real killer? No, it had to be him. It had to.

There was silence as neither of the men spoke. They stood motionless and glared at each other, sizing each other up the way they did in western movies during a showdown. Matt had that part right.

Bill took two steps toward Devon.

"Don't try anything funny," Devon shouted. "I'm the one holding the knife. Remember? Now give me the—"

Bill growled and swooped down on Devon. The men struggled, rolling over on the dusty concrete floor, the knife flying through the air. Devon landed a punch to Bill's face, but he was no match for the heftier and much stronger man.

My heart pounded as the scene unfolded on the screen.

A gunshot cracked through the air. Devon collapsed.

"He shot Devon!" I screamed in horror.

40

———

The sound of the gunshot echoed in my mind. That Bill had planned to kill Devon all along was a startling turn of events.

"Wait here, Amber!" Ryan sprang out of the car and dashed toward the building, entering through the side door.

I looked back at the screen. Devon lay prone, unmoving. Bill was nowhere in sight.

I peered through the darkness. Vague outlines along the perimeter of the building confirmed that police officers were entering through the side door.

A shadowy form crossed in front of the car. A grunt preceded a hard thump beside me. Ryan was back.

No...it wasn't Ryan!

Bill slithered into the driver's seat and pointed a handgun at me. "Ready to go for a ride, little lady?"

The negative energy surrounding him intruded into my space like a blast of black smoke. The dark was too much to handle. I didn't move. If he shot Devon so easily, he wouldn't hesitate to shoot me. And yet...

"You won't need this." He snatched the laptop and flung it to the back seat. He switched the gun to his left hand, then started the ignition with his right hand and drove off.

It was my chance. I grasped the handle on the passenger side to make my escape. Better to throw myself out of a moving vehicle than risk getting shot.

Bill gripped my left arm. I struggled to break free, but he yanked me back inside. A hard click sounded as the doors locked.

"Stay put, Amber," Bill shouted. "You're my insurance."

"You won't get far." I tried to sound confident. "The police have surrounded the place."

"They won't be looking for this unmarked car, will they?" he sneered. He transferred the gun to his right hand and pointed it inches away from me.

Ryan's car radio signaled an incoming message. He'd reported his car was stolen. I didn't dare lower my guard. Sitting next to a killer, I sensed the worst wasn't over yet.

Bill gunned the engine, and we raced down the road toward the main street. I peered into the darkness, searching for signs of a police cruiser or armed officers. Nothing.

Then two police cruisers darted out of nowhere. They crossed our path and came to a shrieking stop.

Bill stepped on the brakes and veered but couldn't stop in time. I raised my arms to cover my face a split second before we slammed into the cars. Our airbags deployed and pinned us against our seats.

Sirens blared and tires screeched, jerking me out of a dreamlike state. The outdoors lit up with blinding light, and I shielded my eyes against the brightness.

I sensed movement beside me. Bill was emerging from an unconscious state. His gun hung limply in his hand.

I attempted to wrestle it out of his hand. He held on tight and fired a shot, the bullet piercing the roof of the car.

The driver's car door swung open. A familiar voice shouted, "Get your hands up where I can see them!" *Matt!*

He yanked Bill out of his seat, forcing him to the ground. Two other officers restrained Bill and seized his gun. The click of handcuffs meant he was no longer a threat.

The passenger door opened, and Matt peeked into the car. "You okay, Amber?"

"Uh-huh," I said. "Yes."

He held out a hand to help me step out.

I staggered into streams of light from police cruisers bordering us. The impact of the deployed airbags hadn't affected me as badly this time. My face suffered burns that would heal in time. My legs, though, were shaking from the ordeal. I held onto the car door to steady myself.

Ryan reached my side in the next moment. "Thank goodness you're okay," he whispered, holding me close to him. Not wanting to attract undue attention, he swiftly released me.

Uniformed police escorted Bill Hardy into the back seat of a cruiser. His nose was bloody and, as he turned to look at me, his piercing stare sent chills up and down my spine.

My gaze shifted to the attendants who wheeled Devon on a stretcher trolley into a waiting ambulance. A black haze enveloped him like a transparent cloak. I'd experienced a similar vision before. It was a sign Devon was near death.

EPILOGUE

Devon Hill didn't regain consciousness. He died days after he was shot. He'd accomplished what he'd promised: He'd agreed to help us, no matter the risks, and unwittingly sacrificed his life in the process.

Bill Hardy's court date would decide his future. Although his lawyer claimed that he acted in self-defense when he shot Devon, our video evidence indicated otherwise. It meant Bill could spend the rest of his life in jail. Call it karma.

As for who would get the official title of serial killer, that decision was determined the day Devon and Bill faced off in the abandoned building. During a search of Devon's apartment, the police discovered a sealed envelope under his mattress. Inside were three matchbooks from The Silver Anchor. Forensics confirmed that the fingerprints on the matchbooks belonged to Devon Hill. Three matches had been removed from each matchbook. The three matches left at each crime scene corresponded to the ones torn off in the respective matchbooks found under Devon's mattress. That he'd taken out his anger on Susan after he learned she was pregnant with Bill's baby was the basis for the first of his revenge killings. Ryan theorized that personal rejection provoked the next two murders, that of Michelle Roy and Pamela Cooper.

Police inspected the car that Devon had borrowed from a so-called friend to drive to his meeting with Bill. It had a broken headlight and dents in the front bumper. Forensics determined that scratches on the car had residue paint in a gray shade that matched the paint on my car. The fragment of a headlight retrieved from my accident corresponded to a missing piece of the headlight on the car that Devon had driven. Forensics found traces of blood on the bumper that proved the same car had been involved in the incident that struck and killed Nadia's boyfriend.

In a conclusive note that revealed the identity of my attacker, police traced the ownership of the car to Devon Hill. Records indicated that Devon had taken possession of the car from its original owner days after we reopened Susan's cold case. Ryan theorized that Devon's drug habit had extended beyond personal use and that he'd acquired the car from a "friend" in exchange for a delivery of drugs.

With the elimination of threats to the unit, the capture of a serial killer, and the closure of three cold cases days before Christmas, Lieutenant Payton couldn't stop bragging about our achievements to his counterparts. His admiration knew no bounds as we gathered in his office for an informal Christmas celebration. He praised the team members for their efforts, including the speed at which they'd uploaded the paper case files to the database.

Matt astonished me when he said, "Lieutenant, about the three cold cases. If Amber hadn't shared her insights with us and steered us toward the serial killer theory, we wouldn't be here today." He raised his glass in a toast. "Here's to Amber."

The team cheered and raised their glasses in my honor. Their appreciation overwhelmed me, especially when Nadia walked over and hugged me. I grew teary and blamed the wine.

"I'm pleased to announce more good news," the lieutenant

said. "An increased budget has been approved for the new year, which means the addition of investigators to the team."

"Here's to solving more cold cases!" Ryan said.

More cheers followed. Best wishes were exchanged before we all left for a short but well-deserved break.

Ryan and I spent the Christmas holidays celebrating with family and friends. I even introduced Ryan to Nicole when she invited us to her place for dinner. I wasn't surprised to discover she'd been dating that single dad who she'd claimed wasn't interested in her. So much for secret relationships.

ACKNOWLEDGMENTS

Silent Night: A Christmas Mystery is the third book in the Amber McNeil Mystery series. Like the first two books, this cold-case mystery features a twisted, fairy-tale influence on a modern crime and the ongoing battle between good and evil.

I am grateful to the beta readers, editor, proofreaders, and cover designer who contributed valuable comments along the way. My gratitude extends to my family and friends who continue to encourage and support me during my writing journey.

My appreciation also goes to readers and booksellers who make it all happen. Your interest in my work motivates me to keep on writing.

ABOUT THE AUTHOR

Sandra Nikolai is the author of the Megan Scott/Michael Elliott Mystery series and the Amber McNeil Mystery series. In addition to her novels, Sandra has published a string of short crime stories, garnering awards along the way.

A graduate of McGill University in Montreal, Sandra held jobs in sales, finance, and high tech before leaving the corporate world to pursue a career in writing. She likes to think that plotting a whodunit reveals the lighter—yet more mysterious—side of her persona.

Visit www.sandranikolai.com and sign up for Sandra's quarterly newsletter to get news on book releases, exclusive offers, and other inside information. Your email address will never be shared and you can unsubscribe at any time.

You can also find Sandra on social media:

Twitter: twitter.com/SandraNikolai

Facebook: facebook.com/SandraNikolaiAuthor

Instagram: instagram.com/sandranikolaiauthor

ALSO BY SANDRA NIKOLAI

Amber McNeil Mystery series

The Missing Slipper

The Red Hoodie

Megan Scott/Michael Elliott Mystery series

False Impressions

Fatal Whispers

Icy Silence

Dark Deeds

Broken Trust

Cold Revenge

For more details and store links, visit Sandra's Books page on her website at www.sandranikolai.com